The Fingerprint of Faith

DANIEL FULTON

Dedication

I would like to dedicate this book to every teacher I ever had but especially to Mrs. Margaret Wiseman, my 12th grade English teacher who knew of my love of words long before I was willing to admit it to myself.

Contents

CHAPTER 1

In the Beginning Was the Technology

He felt the force of the blast. The invisible shock wave knocked him to the ground, and he was fifty meters away in the woods. He struggled to his feet and ran back to the house. He saw the bodies of his family—his father, his mother, two sisters and brother—charred beyond recognition. The stench of burned flesh was so strong that he vomited until he passed out. He came to, trembling, not wanting to investigate further but drawn to the tragic scene.

There were no first responders or firefighters. Out here in the country, in the middle of Indiana, in the middle of America, it was not unusual for it to take a half hour or more for them to arrive. The house was totally destroyed. Bits and pieces of the roof were scattered in the woods.

The woods behind him were his sanctuary, his place to go when a complex computer problem plagued him. He walked in the starlight or the moonlight in the stillness, disturbed only by the night creatures foraging for food in their eternal quest for survival.

As he investigated the remains of the house, it occurred to him that the blast seemed to originate from his room. There was nothing in there to cause an explosion of such force. His closet was full of clothes, and his room was full of computer gear and all the same things any nineteen-year-old would have.

His room differed only in the fact that his computer equipment was always state of the art. He had graduated from MIT at fifteen. He had already created the most sophisticated and secured blockchain in existence. His grasp of the workings of the blockchain technology and the algorithms needed to make them possible had opened doors.

He'd spent the past three-and-a-half years in the company of high-powered executives in the banking world. The intrigue and greed turned his stomach. Wealth didn't mean much to him. It was nice to buy whatever he wanted, but these people were obsessed with possessing more, for the sake of more. Most of them couldn't possibly spend what they already had in a lifetime.

His family was poor, dedicated missionaries. He identified more with the homeless on the street he saw on his way to the high-powered board meetings than the greedy powerbrokers he was forced to accompany. If he hadn't received a full scholarship to MIT, his life would have been much different.

With the help of his father and some trusted associates, he had established several benevolent companies all over the world. As soon as he could, he turned over the helm of his empire to people who were comfortable in that environment.

He preferred the company of technology to the fickle nuances of people his own age, and people in general. He did take solace in his own family. That is why he still lived at home, even though he was a multibillionaire. He paid off all the family debts and offered to buy them a mansion anywhere they wanted, but they chose to stay in Indiana. He could understand. The extended family was here, and their ministry was everything to them.

He heard sirens in the distance. A neighbor had probably called in the explosion. If the explosion had started in his room, it occurred to him that this was more than an accident. He had ruffled a lot of feathers with his latest blockchain offering. He could securely send any amount of wealth anywhere in the world in nanoseconds. He had made, and was still making, millions on this offering alone. Maybe there were sore losers. The Rothfellas, the wealthiest, most powerful banking family in the world, had invested heavily in the blockchain technology, but his creation made their large fees and slow technology obsolete overnight. What if they held a grudge? All he could think of was to run!

He turned and disappeared into the woods. He threw his cell phone in the creek, after he smashed it on a rock. He knew it could be tracked. He ran to the edge of the woods and crossed into the creek at the edge of the adjoining woods. He ran down the creek until he came to the edge of the road on the next country block. That would throw off the robot hounds, but the heat-seeking, infrared drones would stalk him from the air. He had to get to the truck stop about five kilometers away. There he could blend in with all the other people and stay invisible for a while. He knew the first responders would have to follow protocols, and that would take time. Enough time for him to steal a ride at the truck stop to anywhere but here.

CHAPTER 2

The First Response

Bob Turin was in the first fire truck on the scene. The big tanker was right behind. He jumped out like he had done a thousand times in his career and ran to the scene. He was the man. Every piece of equipment, all the workforce, was in his charge. His training allowed him to make split-second decisions that saved lives and property.

After his military career, this seemed to him a natural progression. He dropped the communicator to his side. There was nothing the firefighters could do. He brought the device back to his mouth and gave the order to stand down. The firefighters would have to stay and comb the woods for hot spots, but he could tell that the house hadn't burned; it exploded. His next call was to the bomb squad. It would have to investigate. He had seen this before in the desert wars.

Whatever device was used exploded with such force that the roof was blown off and the walls collapsed outward all over the property. The people inside were instantly killed. The force of the blast turned their organs to mush, broke all their bones, and seared their flesh beyond recognition. The explosion sucked all the oxygen out of the air, so the burnable material that survived was spared a fire. It seemed to have originated from a bedroom at one end of the house. He got on the phone to the sheriff's office.

The sheriff needed to get detectives out here, pronto, and secure the scene. The sun was just peeking over the trees. That would make the recon in the woods easier. He wondered if the occupant of that bedroom was somewhere else or if the blast had made them disappear. That determination was for the bomb squad. It did seem odd that no trace was found anywhere, at least nothing big enough to see with the naked eye.

The last call, the coroner, was the hardest. He knew the occupants of the house, Alonzo Browning and his family. They were the most unselfish, giving people he knew. Thanks to the Browning Foundation, homelessness didn't exist in this area. The churches all were given the money to minister to everyone, regardless of their background or denomination.

He knew he was jumping to conclusions from a professional standpoint, but he'd talked to Alonzo and his family last evening at Erica's restaurant and was positive they were home last night. He went to high school with Alonzo; they were buddies. He couldn't fathom the idea that someone would want Alonzo dead, let alone his entire family. He sat on the running board of his fire truck with his head buried in his hands. Most of the time, he loved his job, but right now he couldn't stomach it.

The robot hounds arrived. They were programmed to sniff out a suspect as well or better than the real hounds the department used to use. With the change of a computer command, they could go from drug sniffers to cadaver dogs to trackers. They were an indispensable tool for the police department.

The drone squad arrived. It could do in the air what the robots on the ground couldn't. The drones used the latest heat-seeking and infrared detection technology the military had developed for wartime. The two squads worked in unison to pinpoint a subject. If anyone, or his or her remains, were out there, they would locate them. They started with a five-kilometer radius. After that, they would expand to ten and then fifteen until they were certain of the person's whereabouts, dead or alive.

The arson squad, the coroner, the detectives, forensics, and the bomb squad had arrived. Bob was glad that someone could take over. He readied his men to leave. He couldn't wait to get out of there.

CHAPTER 3

The Fugitive

He seemed to have been running forever. His lungs ached, and his face itched from the corn leaves slapping him as he ran. The corn was taller than he was and afforded some cover. One more field and he could see the truck stop. Finally, he was through the last field. He emerged from the corn row, glad for the open air. He bent over and breathed in and out as deeply as he could. He didn't want to alarm anyone at the truck stop by looking like the fugitive he was.

When his pulse and his breathing slowed to normal, he brushed the corn pollen from his hair and clothes and readied for the daunting task of getting across the highway. He saw in the distance the drones with the searchlights stopping and starting as they found deer or coyotes and had to stop to investigate each one. It was hard for them to identify objects in the dense canopy of the trees behind his house. It bought him some time.

He crouched by the roadside, looked both ways, and sprinted to the other side before any headlights appeared. Down the ravine and up the other side he ran. Now the only thing left was to transition to the parking lot and walk nonchalantly into the store. His heart was pounding from the anxiety.

Inside he went straight to the restroom to brush the rest of the corn pollen and dirt off, so he would look presentable. He rinsed out his mouth repeatedly, washed his face, and wiped it dry with paper towels. He walked out into the store.

He tried to think of everything a fugitive would need for survival. He bought jerky and water and trail mix. He bought a hat that said, "LOVE MY TRUCK" and a sweatshirt with a caricature of a Tesla big rig on it. He found a vest with many pockets for his supplies. He hoped that would last him until he found a library with a computer.

When he got to the checkout, there were four people ahead of him. He patiently waited his turn. He swallowed hard, hoping for anonymity as he laid his selections on the counter. He had tried to hide from the store cameras by following someone much taller than he was to the checkout. He put the bit-card in the slot after the robot scanned the items.

He put the hat on as soon as the robot cashier completed the transaction and slung the clothing over his shoulder and walked out. The first traces of daylight were breaking as he walked among the many trucks parked on the huge back lot. Some were driverless now, but the Teamsters union had put up such a fight, that most still had token drivers.

The trucks could travel twenty-four hours a day without any break, except to recharge. He walked down the line until he came to a flatbed with two large culverts strapped on its trailer side by side, creating a triangle-shaped void between them at the base. He walked on by and looked for any sign of the driver or any security cameras. When the coast was clear, he walked between the flatbed and the large cargo truck parked beside it. In one motion, he hopped up on to the trailer and slid into the area between the metal culverts. He settled in for what he knew was going to be a long, hard trip.

Oh, how he wished he could have just gotten in his new Tesla and programmed it to go wherever he wanted, like he usually did. He could have had his favorite music blaring and kicked back in luxury. Those days were gone until he could sort out this nightmare. His car could be tracked. He purposely left his bit-card in the trash as he walked out, because he knew it had tracking software. In one instant, he had gone from one of the richest men in the country to a homeless and broke derelict.

All the cameras he had personally placed around the house and the property would tell the story. When he got where he was going, wherever that was, he would go to the nearest library and hack into his system. He knew that the library computers were never state of the art, but he would have to make do. The police would be able to get into the "official" security cameras, but no one knew about his personal cameras.

He felt the robot attendant unhook the charger and the driver climb in and shut the door. The behemoth slowly rolled out to the highway. The lights of the truck lit the way; they were for the benefit of the travelers on the highway. The self-driving software didn't rely on visual. It was guided by satellite to the highway where a guidance system imbedded in the road kept it in line until it was time to exit to another highway or to its destination.

Once the truck got into the flow of traffic and settled in to the appointed speed in its designated lane, David relaxed. As far as the eye could see in the minutes before dawn, were the trucks. They were delegated to one lane now, there was no passing. They traveled together in single file, resembling a line of ants following their invisible trail to the colony.

CHAPTER 4

The Detectives

The crime scene tape was in place when the car pulled up. The whole property resembled a war zone. The forensics technicians were everywhere, taking pictures and collecting evidence. One of them motioned the detectives over. When they got to the tech, he motioned at the ground.

Dan Bolker had been a detective for a long time, but he had never seen such a devastated crime scene. His partner, Justin Peters, and he exchanged glances when they got out of the car.

"What have you got?" Bolker asked as he reached the tech.

"Looks like someone came up on the sight of this devastation and lost their lunch. The robot dogs have been here and followed the scent into the woods where it ended in the creek. It seems like someone was in a hurry to get away and didn't want us to follow."

"Have the drones found anything yet?" Peters asked.

"Not yet. They are expanding the search now. The main highway is five kilometers from here. There's a truck stop down there. If the subject got that far, he could have caught a ride to anywhere."

"Ok, keep us informed."

"Will do. By the way, there are six people listed who live here and only five body bags."

"Oh, thanks for the info," Bolker acknowledged.

The wheels were already turning in his head. A new Tesla was in the drive. It had collateral damage from the blast. It was registered to David Browning. The car was still drivable in Bolker's opinion. Why didn't David take his car?

"Detectives, we are positive the vomit belongs to the oldest boy, David. We found his smashed phone in the creek and evidence he has been in the woods numerous times. Fingerprints on the phone and a rock near it are his," said Don Hinders, head of the forensics team.

Why would David feel like he had to run? thought Bolker. *We need to talk to him as a person of interest.*

"Peters, I think we need to issue an APB for David Browning as a person of interest. It seems to me that he left in a hurry for some unknown reason. It's as good a place to start as any. I think we also need to talk to anyone who has been on or near this property for the past week to see if we can find motive and method for this."

"Yeah, I noticed lots of cameras on the property. Maybe we can get the tech gurus to unlock their secrets. Surely some of them recorded the blast."

"Ok, let's get to it."

The techs received the data from the cameras in record time. It seemed this was going to be a high-priority, high-profile case. They reduced the files to fifteen minutes before and after the explosion. The two detectives poured over them to try to fill in the gaps in the timeline with the events leading to the explosion. Some of the cameras didn't show the explosion. They didn't seem to be working at the time under investigation. This was a state-of-the-art system, so that seemed strange. Those that did work showed the intense blast.

One minute, the house was there, and the next it wasn't. The intense fireball damaged the trees in the yard for 30 meters around the house. The cameras in the tree line in the woods behind the house showed the shadow of an intense orange glow before the blast. But all the cameras in the front that could have seen it directly were disabled. The techs needed to check this security company out.

"Ultimate Security, how can we help you?" said the computer-generated voice. The detective was prompted through all the selections in the company menu. How he hated these things. It seemed that after all the selections were exhausted, he still ended up talking to a computer, and sometimes he couldn't tell the voice from a real person. After many minutes, he finally navigated his way through all the choices and got to a person.

"This is Alvin Hinn, owner and CEO of Ultimate Security, how can I help you?"

"Did you say owner?" the detective asked.

"Yes, sir! I'm the only person needed here. Except for field technicians, everything is run by computer and robots! I saw you were identified as a detective from Hamilton County, Indiana. I read all the detective stuff I can get my hands on. I'm a crime scene buff."

Oh, great, thought the detective one of *those.*

If there was anything he hated worse than all the jobs that had been replaced by computers, it was the amateur detective trying to tell him his job. He supposed it was just a matter of time before he was replaced too. Five more years, that's all he needed to get his pension, five more years.

"We subpoenaed records of the cameras at the Alonzo Browning residence at 6210 South, 59200 East, Hamilton County, Indiana. We have a few questions about some of the cameras that seem to be offline, specifically the ones facing the front bedroom."

"I'll check; let me pull them up. The night in question was August twelfth of this year, right? And the week prior also?"

"Yes."

"My records show that the cameras were working fine, in fact, we had just sent a technician out to check everything on the tenth of the month, like we do every month, as part of the premium package that the family purchased. I'll check with the technician, but everything checked out, as far as I know."

"Get back to me after you talk to the tech, will you?"

"Of course. They were good clients; I hated to lose them, I'm sorry our cameras didn't help you."

Peters had been eavesdropping on the conversation. When the guy mentioned the technician, he started typing furiously on his computer.

"Hey, Bolker, look at this!" he said.

"What have you got?" Bolker asked.

He knew by the tone of Peter's voice, he had something. They had been partners for a long time. Peters was a bloodhound, sniffing out clues that no one else could.

"You remember when we interviewed the retired lady next door, the one who called in the explosion? She said she saw the van checking the cameras on the tenth, which wasn't unusual because it comes every month. The unusual thing is she claims that the van came back the next day, on the eleventh. She just thought that the

THE FINGERPRINT OF FAITH

tech had to come back and repair something he found from the previous day."

"Maybe we need to talk to the neighbor again and bring in the tech at the security place and talk to him." Peters was out the door before Bolker finished talking.

—◊—

Peters walked into the office after the second interview with the neighbor. By the look on his face, Bolker knew he had uncovered pertinent information.

"The second visit I told you about was a different guy than the previous day, according to the neighbor. She recognized the first guy; he also checked her security on a regular basis. But the second man on the trip the next day was much larger; she didn't recognize him."

"You gotta love nosey neighbors!" grinned Bolker.

CHAPTER 5

David's Anguish

He had overestimated the comfort level of his ride. The culverts swayed in the wind, singing a mournful tune on occasion, when the wind was just right. The tie-down straps strained with every pitch and yaw of the truck. The culverts were giant megaphones making every sound as loud as a rock concert. Every bump in the road transferred directly to his spine. He rolled up his sweatshirt for a makeshift pillow and lay on his back with his hat over his face. Tears leaked out of his eyes and down his temples onto his makeshift pillow as he wrestled with his new reality.

Why? Why? Why? When he got settled into wherever he was going, he would launch his own investigation. The cameras would tell the story. He felt lonesome like he had never felt before. His family was always his sanctuary; his father his rock, his financial advisor, and mentor. He started to remember his childhood.

At three, his father recognized his extraordinary relationship with the computer. His dad bought him an iPad with all the children's Bible stories and the games appropriate for his age. He also downloaded the entire Bible. By five, David had memorized the entire Bible. His father was so proud.

David was quite the little celebrity. He had even been on National Christian TV. The host picked a random Bible verse, and David recited it word for word. A smile graced his face through the tears. He remembered when at ten he had hacked into the app store and downloaded all the apps and games he wanted for free. When his dad found out, he made David get a job with his farmer friend down the road, cleaning out the hog barn after the long winter.

The farmer had a robot to do the job, but David had to do it by hand with a pitchfork. It was hard, smelly work, but he stuck with it. He had to do this until he made enough money to pay for all the apps and games. He also got grounded for a month with no computer. That's when he learned to appreciate the beauty and solace of the woods around his house. He had nothing else to do but roam the woods until his purgatory was over.

As part of his probation, at the end of his grounding, he had to work as a consultant for the security firm that handled the security for the app store. The techs couldn't believe a ten-year-old kid breached all the levels of their security. Of course, his father made him give the considerable amount of money he was paid to a local charity. He wasn't allowed to profit from his crime.

David's thoughts were interrupted, as the truck seemed to be slowing. He hoped it was stopping. The rumbling ride had been complicated by the fact he had to find a toilet really bad. Every bump was now agony.

The truck pulled into a charging station and stopped. When the driver got out and the robot hooked up the charger, he crawled out of his lair and looked for cameras and drones. When the coast was clear, he made a beeline to the restroom! He started to unzip as soon as he got to the urinal. He fumbled around and got situated just as his stream started. His eyes rolled in the back of his head, the sheer ecstasy of making it in time caused an audible, involuntary moan. The guy next to him turned his head in David's direction, a clear violation of restroom etiquette. It was always eyes straight ahead at the urinal. David didn't notice.

When he finished and was at the sink washing his hands, the guy asked, "Didn't I see you back at the last stop in Indiana? You look too young to be a driver. Are you traveling with family?"

"No! And it's none of your business where I've been or where I'm going!" David hissed back at the guy. The remark about family hit him the wrong way.

"No offense intended," the guy said, "just being friendly. There's no one to talk to in the truck. The radio and the monitor movies get old. There's no one to talk to on the phone at night except other truckers."

The driver knew he'd seen the kid at the Indiana stop. He walked around a while before he went back to his truck to login and catch up on his computer work. It would take an hour for his rig to recharge, and he wanted to figure out why he was showing an extra 160 pounds on the computer. Because the trucks didn't have to take on diesel fuel, the new technology allowed for pinpoint weights and eliminated the need to go through weight scales. He got out his tool to tighten the straps and went around checking each one. A monkey, or a robot, could do his job now. If it hadn't been for the political clout of the Teamsters union, he and every other truck driver would have been replaced a long time ago.

When he strolled around the back of the trailer, something caught his eye between the two large culverts he was carrying. He didn't stop; he continued to go around the truck, checking the straps. When he got back to the cab on the driver's side, he threw the tool in the toolbox a lot harder than he needed to as a diversion and jumped on the front of the trailer, hoping to catch who or whatever was between the load. He reached between the culverts and came out with a handful of shirt attached to the kid at the urinal. He put his free hand around the kid's throat, so he wouldn't get any ideas about trying to run.

His nose was close to the kid's face, when he asked in his best drill-sergeant voice, "What are you doing on my truck?!"

David couldn't breathe, let alone answer. His toes were barely touching the trailer floor. He felt the power of the large hand around his neck and saw out of the corner of his eye the Semper Fi tattoo on the guy's arm and decided to not try to anything. As he relaxed, so did the hand.

"You don't look like you're homeless to me, so what are you doing on my truck?" asked the trucker again.

"Someone blew my house up and killed my whole family. I think they were after me," he blurted out.

The driver had heard the story on the morning news. He relaxed his iron grip.

"According to the news, the police only want to talk to you as a person of interest. Why don't you give yourself up?"

"I don't trust the police or the media anymore. The people who are after me are very powerful and can buy whatever loyalty they need. You gonna turn me in?"

"I don't know yet. You messed up my log with your extra weight, so I have to find a way to justify that."

"I can fix that easy enough, if you let me see your log pad. There has to be a way to justify extra weight when these big trucks travel in rain or snow. I'm now just a snowflake," he said with a grin, trying to dissipate the trucker's anger.

"Ok, you little punk, but if you try anything, I'll drag you to the police kicking and screaming!"

They both climbed into the cab of the truck. David typed a few things on the onboard computer, and the extra pounds went away.

"How'd you do that?" the driver asked. He was beginning to like this kid.

"That's what I do. I work with computers. I'm a genius when it comes to this kind of stuff. I made some really powerful people mad by writing a program that caused them to lose a lot of money, and now they want me dead. They were willing to go after my whole family to get to me."

David didn't know how much the trucker knew about blockchain and the workings of the bitcoin economy, so he made his explanation simple.

The trucker said, "Come into the truck stop with me so I can keep an eye on you and get something to eat."

"I can't; if someone recognizes me, I'm done."

"What makes you think I won't turn you in?"

"I don't know if you will or not, but if you do, I'll eventually end up dead. I'm not one hundred percent sure of who's out to get me, but I've got a gut feeling. I just need time to prove it. Besides, I don't have a bit-card. I threw it in the trash back in Indiana. The officials can track every time and place the card was used."

The kid was smart, and besides he didn't like the government or the police or anyone in authority much either. He was curious about the kid now, and it'd be nice to have someone to talk to for a change, thought the trucker. *Besides, the kid could fix his log pad for him.*

"I tell you what; I'm going in to get something to eat. If you want to run, you can. I guess you'll just have to trust that I'm not going to turn you in."

The trucker opened the door and went back into the truck stop.

David thought about his next move. It sure would be nice to ride in the cab instead of the trailer. The guy knew too much now. Maybe he would turn him in for spite if he ran. David had been awake for a long time, and his brain was foggy. If he didn't get some rest soon, he would probably make a fatal mistake. He sat on the seat with his head buried in his hands. He must have dozed off, because when the trucker opened the door and climbed in, he jumped. The trucker threw a bag at him. He caught it by reflex.

"What's this?" he asked.

"I thought you might be hungry," he said, as he handed David his soft drink.

David opened the bag and devoured the burger and fries without taking a breath, or so it seemed to the driver. He smiled as he remembered his own son, who was eighteen when he left for the Marines. He went to fight for his country in another one of those seemingly endless and pointless desert wars and came home in a flag-draped coffin five years ago. There wasn't a day that went by that he didn't think of him. Maybe that's why he didn't turn this kid in. He'd had enough of young people dying. He didn't want to be a party to death anymore. The truck pulled out of the lot.

"Name's Jackson Tanner, Jake for short," the trucker said as he extended the same meaty hand that had once been around David's neck.

"David Browning," he returned the introduction.

"You the David Browning who started the Browning Foundation?"

"Yes, that's me."

"Wow, I've got a genuine celebrity in my truck, a real billionaire celebrity! No wonder you fixed my computer so easy!"

David was blushing and squirming in his seat. He never was comfortable with people calling him that.

"You have any kids, Mr. Tanner?"

"First, call me Jake. Second, yes, I have two kids—a girl who's married and has three kids and my boy, Gregg, who died in the war five years ago."

"I'm sorry," David's voice trailed off. He was really getting to like this Jake Tanner. After all, he saved him from a lot of grief and even possibly being arrested as a fugitive.

"What's your story, David?"

The food, the power nap, and being nineteen, that's all it took to rejuvenate David. When Jake asked him that question, he started talking nonstop about everything. From the Bible verses when he was a child, to the powerful Rothfellas and the blockchain that he had developed, and then the explosion and the flight through the fields and why he chose the truck with the two culverts.

When he got to the part about the Bible verses, Jake interrupted, "Are you a Christian, David?"

David shrugged his shoulders, "I don't know. My dad and my whole family were Christians and look where it got them."

"If you don't know, then the answer is no, you're not."

"Are you?" David inquired.

"Yes, I am. It's the only way I got through the loss of my son; the only way I can cope with the crazy things that are going on in this country politically right now; and the only way I can cope with this mundane, boring job. Jesus Christ is my rock and my salvation."

David was silent for a while before he resumed his life story, pondering what Jake had revealed to him in the back of his mind as he talked. He couldn't understand why he was talking so much to a complete stranger, especially because he was trying to remain invisible. When he had finally gotten all the way to sitting in the front of the truck in the present, he stopped talking. His eyes were getting heavy, and his head was bobbing.

"Get in the sleeper and get some shuteye," Jake commanded as he nudged his shoulder.

"Ok." David didn't argue. He was totally spent.

The kilometers rolled by as David slept. Jake mulled over the tale that he had just heard. He'd always thought that money would bring happiness, that is, until he was converted. He guessed this was God's way of showing him that the rich and powerful pay a price for the pursuit of happiness too.

He felt a kinship with David. Maybe it was just the loss of his son. He didn't know, but he felt compelled to help him. He knew how hard it was to lose one child, but he couldn't fathom losing his whole family. He heard the kid moaning and thrashing around in a nightmarish sleep.

He thought back on the good times with his kids when they were small. The laughter they shared at the table as a family came to mind, laughter about the most trivial things. His wife sometimes laughed to tears over something Gregg said. He missed that laughter. He hadn't been able to laugh for five years.

David was stirring. He lay on his back, staring at the ceiling in the sleeper. He heard the constant hum of the electric motors and felt the vibration through the bunk. The tires sang their mournful tune on their endless trek doing the bidding of the satellite and the roadbed overlords. He was forming his plan of attack in his head.

First, David Browning had to disappear. Then he would have to assume an alias.

Because social security numbers had been replaced with a thirty-two-digit password and thumbprint, he would have to somehow link his thumbprint with a new password. The corner of his mouth turned up slightly as he thought of the software programs and the blockchain he'd been involved with. No one knew about the fingerprint link he'd imbedded in each thing he'd ever written.

With the help of a startup company in Nevada that developed a silicone product that looked like paper but was made of silica, he could produce a film that fit over his fingers that recorded his fingerprints with every stroke. Every one of his programs had a back-door security code that only he could access, recognized only by his fingerprint. Hacking the programs would be easy. He crawled back to his seat in the truck.

"Good evening, sleeping beauty," Tanner said sarcastically.

David looked at him, puzzled.

"Sleeping Beauty was an old fable made famous by Walt Disney."

"Who's Walt Disney?" David asked.

Jake forgot that this new generation grew up on an entirely different set of stories than he did. Walt Disney had been replaced by government-sanctioned fairy tales that steered the children to think and act the way they wanted.

"Never mind, that was before your time. So, you know the whole Bible, huh?"

"Yep, ask me anything."

"Ok, Ezekiel 2:1."

David immediately replied, "And he said unto me, Son of man, stand upon thy feet, and I will speak unto thee."

"Right! Ok, how about Job 30:13?"

"They mar my path, they set forward my calamity, they have no helper."

"Right again."

Tanner quizzed him for about a half hour. David didn't miss one. Finally, Jake looked at him in amazement. "You know the Bible front and back and you aren't a Christian?"

"It's just rote memory," said David, "I don't know what most of those words mean."

"Where are we?"

"We're halfway between St. Louis and Kansas City. We'll stop one more time before Kansas City. I'll drop off this load in Kansas City and pick up a load of machinery for Albuquerque, New Mexico. It'll take a few hours. Then we're off again."

The truck slowed and pulled into another truck stop to recharge. They both got out and stretched and walked to the restroom. David went straight back to the truck. Jake walked around and stretched. He pondered why this kid was in his life now. It was close to the anniversary of his boy's death. Maybe this was God's way of getting him through this tough time.

He went back inside the store and got some coffee and sipped it slowly as he walked. He would do his best to talk about Jesus to David. He obviously knew the story, but he was too headstrong and independent to really think he needed Jesus. Maybe when the reality of the loss of his family really sunk in, he'd think differently. Jake vowed to do his best to witness to the kid. He felt like he owed it to the kid, the kid's father, and above all, God. He glanced at his watch, the truck should be charged by now. He headed back to the rig and climbed in.

The truck was already unplugged, so he punched in his code and the truck started to roll.

"How far are we from a library? I need to get to a computer."

"You like barbeque? I know a place close to the downtown Kansas City library that has good ribs. We can leave the truck and call a self-drive to take us to the restaurant."

"Sounds good. You can eat, and I'll go to the library and work."

"What about you; aren't you going to eat?"

"No, I'm not hungry yet."

"Suit yourself; maybe you will be by the time we get there."

They talked as the truck ate up the highway. The time went so much faster for Jake than usual. He told a lot of funny family stories and listened as David told his. When David mentioned his family ministry, Jake saw his opening.

"How could you be around such love all your life and not see the way to Jesus?"

David got a distant look on his face and said, "I don't know, I thought someday my father would baptize me into the fold, but I wasn't ready yet. Too late for that now, I guess."

He turned away to hide the tears from Jake and changed the subject. "How am I going to get to the library without being recognized?"

I wouldn't worry so much. People are so plugged in to their phones any more they don't pay attention to their surroundings. Just act natural, you'll be ok. Let me tell you a little trick we used in the service to sneak back into the barracks after curfew when we didn't want to be recognized by the facial recognition software. Take some of that jerky you have in your vest pocket and cut it into pieces. Put the jerky in your cheeks, so they make them look fat. Just don't try to talk much."

The truck left the highway and lumbered down the ramp to the corner of 16th and Iron Street, Kansas City, Missouri. It pulled into the lot and stopped. The robot came out and inspected the load and had Jake sign the paperwork.

"According to dispatch, the truck will be ready in two hours," he said as he pushed a single button on his phone and punched in the address. "The car will be here in about fifteen minutes."

David didn't answer, as he was lost in thought. It would be great to get his hands on a computer again. He was going over the sequence in his mind that he needed to get back on his feet. His father and his financial advisor had insisted that David set up a shell company in Dubai, along with a discreet way to set up accounts for clients to get funds out of the country and back if necessary. A lot of persecuted Christians had been saved from torture and death by this shell company.

The governments all put travel restrictions on everyone. Passports were now a political tool for the elite or a way to extort money to line the pockets of the politicians. This way the Christians who needed help could travel far away from their persecutors. It was getting increasingly difficult to find sanctuary for these people. Christian persecution had reached into every walk of life in every country, even the US.

Jake poked him. "Before we go, give me that ridiculous hat. Talk about a marker. If you bought that in Indiana, the police will know and call it out on your description. Take mine. It's well used and won't attract attention. And don't even think about wearing that sweatshirt! This truck is a Volvo, not a Tesla! That's just downright offensive!" Jake bellowed with a grin on his face.

David smiled at the ribbing he was getting. It was true though; the hat would have attracted attention.

The car arrived, and they climbed in. Jake punched in the address and they pulled out. Traffic wasn't bad, and a half hour later they were at the Barbeque Heaven. About two blocks away was the library.

"You go eat; I'll catch up with you later. I'll walk to the library."

"Suit yourself, meet me back here when you're done, and I'll call another car."

"Ok." David was already walking away.

It felt good to be walking after the long truck ride. He stuck the precut pieces of jerky in his mouth, like Jake suggested. His cheeks did stick out more. The only problem was he started to salivate almost immediately. He had to suck saliva back into his mouth, so he wouldn't drool. He was beginning to wonder if this was a practical joke!

He entered the library and walked past the desk to the computers. He settled in at one that made him the most inconspicuous. He felt good being in his most familiar environment again. His fingers flew over the keyboard as he made the machine do his bidding. He had to stop long enough to get the jerky positioned in his mouth, so he could chew and swallow it. This saliva thing was just too distracting! Besides, he didn't see any cameras inside the building.

He typed frantically. He broke the ancient library security in about two minutes. He entered the passwords and the codes he had committed to memory. He was thankful his father had insisted he learn the codes. He almost blew it off, because he couldn't think

Daniel Fulton

of any scenario where he would need to have them memorized. Was he ever wrong!

He was at the point where he had to enter a name. He stopped. He knew from the start that David Alonzo Browning could no longer exist, but when he disappeared it was the last remnant of his family. The sadness and resentment overwhelmed him. He had to think.

What elias? Not elias, David, alias, dummy. What alias did he want to use? he thought.

Wait a minute. Elias, hmmm, not bad. Elias, Elias Tobias. Now all he needed was a last name. Montague, yeah. Elias Tobias Montague had a nice ring to it.

Elias Tobias Montague was born. He used the birth date already chosen at random by the computer program. He was from Ames, Iowa, and he was twenty-one. His code was displayed on the screen, so he added his thumbprint. He memorized the code and closed his new identity, double-checking to make sure he had followed all the protocols, so no one could hack in behind him. Now he had to make David disappear. This was going to be much harder.

He couldn't possibly think of every time he had to use his identity. He had birth records, high school records, college records, and records he hadn't thought of that he would have to expunge. He created software that infected every computer or database that contained his code. Again, he typed frantically. He'd been at the computer for an hour. He looked around carefully to see if anyone was paying any attention to him. He still seemed to be anonymous. He went back to his typing. When he had created the program, he double-checked his thought process and his typing. Any time anyone accessed David's information, the program would delete his data.

32

Satisfied that he covered all possibilities, he had one more keystroke to start the process to kill David. He hesitated; his hand began to shake as he remembered what he had been through. His father always told him that life can change in an instant. He was right again. This was like pulling the trigger on a gun. The last of his family would disappear from the face of the earth. It would take his program weeks to do its work, instead of the instant that made his whole family perish. Rage welled inside him as he punched the key way too hard.

He gathered his things to leave. He didn't bother wiping fingerprints. By the time anyone would ever check, his prints would belong to Elias. He was running out of time. He would have to wait for another opportunity to hack his camera information.

CHAPTER 6

Elias Tobias

He had to find a drugstore. He saw a CVS about five blocks away. He went up to the kiosk where bit-cards were issued and typed in his new code. His blockchain made banks obsolete. Any banking could be done online securely with the click of a mouse. He went through the prompts, hesitating only when asked to put his thumbprint on the screen.

"Here goes!" he whispered.

The machine hesitated for a minute. The screen lit up with "WELCOME, ELIAS TOBIAS MONTAGUE. HOW CAN I HELP YOU?" He typed in an exorbitant amount of bitcoin just to see if it would go through. Fifty-thousand bitcoin would last the average family of four for over five years at the current valuation. He grinned inwardly.

I'm back! he thought.

He went to the aisle where hair color was located and picked out the reddest red. He went to the area by the pharmacy and got some gel-filled toothache pads that went in the mouth and released medication slowly. He didn't take them out of the plastic packing before he stuffed them into his mouth. He went to the checkout counter and handed the robot the toothache pad box with the barcode and the hair color box. He swiped his bit-card and paid the bill. It worked; he was able to pay his own way again. He ran back past the library toward the restaurant. Jake was waiting outside.

"Where've you been?" he asked.

"I went to the drugstore down the street to get some stuff after I was done at the library. I have a new bit-card now, so I can pay my own way."

"That's great, but I was about to leave without you. It's been over two hours. The only reason I didn't is because a car wasn't available."

It pulled in the lot just as Jake finished his admonishment.

"Sorry, Jake, I'll get a new cell phone when we get to New Mexico, so I can keep in touch."

They piled in the car and headed back to the truck. On the way, Jake got a text telling him the truck was ready.

"Good barbeque?" David (Elias) asked. He'd have to continue to be David to Jake Tanner.

"Yep, as usual."

Jake was glad that David made it back in time. He'd enjoyed being around a young person again. Especially this one; he seemed to have his head on straight, even if he was a genius. Jake was glad he didn't have to drive tonight. He was sleepy after that big meal and just wanted to crawl into the sleeper.

They rode back mostly in silence. When they pulled in the lot, the truck had been charged and the huge machine was loaded. Jake walked around the truck and checked the straps on the load. Everything seemed fit for travel, so he climbed into the cab and punched in the location. David crawled on to the seat beside him. The truck started to roll.

"I'm gonna get some sleep," Jake declared as he crawled into the sleeper. "Night all."

David was left to his thoughts. He dozed some, but just as sleep would almost come he would hear the explosion again, and he was back in the Indiana woods running toward the house. He wondered if he would ever truly sleep again. He planned his next moves in his head. He would have to get a place to stay and rebuild his computer equipment back to his demanding standards. Then he could track down who took away his whole life.

He wouldn't be able to go back to his family's funeral. He would have to mourn silently, from a distance. The anger welled inside. Whoever did this was going to pay!

He watched the scenery as the truck rolled out of Kansas City through the seemingly endless rolling Kansas fields. Huge machines were crawling over the landscape harvesting the grain, causing clouds of dust to rise into the sky, turning the sunset red. There was not a human in sight. Everything was automated. Humans were increasingly isolated from life, holed up in cages they called home, watching TV or the internet, being spoonfed what the government wanted them to think and know.

He hadn't been gone twenty-four hours yet, but how he missed his hundred-acre woods and the solitude it afforded. The sun disappeared, leaving the truck caravan in the glow of the moon and the stars. One by one, the truck lights turned on in the darkness, lighting their progress over the endless trail as far as David could see forward or back.

The kilometers and the minutes rolled on. He nodded off, trying to think of happy times. The truck stops all looked the same, only the scenery changed. He really enjoyed the stories Jake told of family and of his time in the service and even when he tried to steer the conversation to God.

Right now, though, he was really angry with God. No matter how he tried to rationalize what happened, he always came back to the fact that his family died, and God could have prevented it! If the Rothfellas were behind this, and he was almost certain they were, they were going to be sorry!

The truck pulled into Albuquerque in the late afternoon. It pulled up to the charger and stopped. Jake updated his log. He got some bad news; the next load wouldn't be ready until morning. He was hoping to get home soon. He didn't like leaving his wife alone on the anniversary of the death of their son. No matter what day of the week it was, they went to church and prayed together. He could still make it; he'd just be cutting it close. He'd learned a long time ago to just trust in God and keep the wheels turning.

"Hey, David, we need to find a place to stay tonight. There's a hotel about five kilometers away that has a pretty good restaurant. I'll get us a car ordered."

"Ok," said David. It would be nice to try to sleep without the truck sounds constantly in his ears. The car whisked them to the hotel. Jake checked them in while David stayed in the car. He came out with the security cards and grabbed his bag. All David had was a sack with the stuff he'd bought in Kansas City. The car left, and they walked in silence to the room.

When the door swung open, the smell of stale, antiseptic air hit them. It was clean but sparse, not like the Trump Tower rooms he was used to. Those days were over, at least for a while.

Jake tossed his bag on the first bed, so David walked around him to the second bed. Jake turned on the TV and started flipping through the channels.

After a few minutes of not finding anything to watch, Jake said, "I'm ready to eat. You coming?"

"No, I'm going to get cleaned up. I smell, and I'm just beat. Leave the TV on. Just bring me back a couple of tacos and sweet tea."

"Ok, I'll be back in about an hour."

When Jake left, he went toward the bathroom, past the vanity with the wall-to-wall mirror. He didn't recognize himself at first. He had started growing his beard on his eighteenth birthday, his emancipation day. It was matted with the residue of tears and dirt from the road. His eyes had bags under them from lack of sleep, and his eyelids were swollen. He hadn't had enough water to drink, and his skin was pale and dehydrated. He looked like he had aged ten years in less than two days.

He headed for the shower with the box of hair color in his hand. He read the instructions and tossed the box in the sink. He fiddled with the shower until the water was just right and stepped in. He let the hot water wash over him for a few minutes before he even moved. He felt the tension in his muscles melt away. Then lathering up, he washed all the road grime away. If only he could wash his grief away.

After he had relaxed for a while, he grabbed the hair color and followed the directions on the package. He put the color in the bottle and shook it for a minute, like the instructions indicated, and then smeared it on his head. He put the plastic cap on his head. The solution slightly burned his scalp. He put the leftover liquid on his beard.

David dressed and sat on the edge of his bed. He had fifteen minutes to endure for the color to work, so he started channel surfing. He stopped abruptly on the evening news channel. There was a picture of his house, or where his house had been, and the news story. At the end of the story was a picture of him.

It was a Photoshopped picture that didn't show the scar on his forehead, where he ran into a door at the age of twelve and had to have stitches. He also had a birthmark on his left cheek that didn't appear in the photo, and he didn't have a beard. His mother had insisted on the cosmetic retouches in this college graduation picture.

I love you, Mother! he thought. Most of the stuff on the computer was destroyed in the blast, and it would take a while for anyone to hack into the cloud and retrieve his data. Maybe if he got set up with a new computer soon enough, he could go in and modify his pictures.

Suddenly, he couldn't take it anymore! He had to get the hair color off his face and scalp. He undressed, turned on the shower, got back in, and washed the color down the drain. He rinsed and rinsed. That red stained everything! Maybe he should have gone blond. Finally, he was finished. He looked in the mirror and studied the face staring back.

It was red all right. Irish red, almost orange! His stubble was tinted but not nearly as much. All in all, it looked ok, kind of modern and chic. He was nineteen, he could pull it off. He was sitting on the edge of the bed channel surfing when the door latch clicked, and Jake walked in.

"What happened to your hair?" he asked. "Your hair looks like the bottom end of an orangutan!"

David grinned sheepishly. "Part of my disguise. I just saw a picture on the news of me, and I think I look different enough to fool most people now. Besides, this can't be any more stupid than putting beef jerky in my cheeks. I think you were messing with me!"

Jake had a gleam in his eye, and his body language gave him away. "I wouldn't do anything like that to you! Here's your food. I'm going to take a shower and get some sleep."

David was mindlessly clicking the remote, his thoughts randomly skirting his new reality. When Jake got out of the shower, he walked over to his bag and took out his personal pad. He sat down at the desk and began to read. Curiosity got the best of David.

"What are you reading?"

"I'm reading my daily devotional and praying."

"You can still pray after God let your son die?" David asked incredulously.

"Yes," replied Jake. "You see, I don't know the why, but I know God is still in control, and I have to have faith that he knows the reason, even if I can't begin to comprehend."

It was too soon after the tragedy for David to even comprehend Jake's last statement. He couldn't think of God without indignation welling up inside him. He continued to channel surf in silence. Jake went back to his studies. He knew exactly where David was. He'd been there himself. He said a silent prayer for the kid.

David had clicked on every channel at least five times. He knew there wasn't anything he wanted to watch, but he was afraid to go to bed and shut his eyes. In the truck, he had the excuse for not being able to sleep because of all the road noise and movement.

He knew deep down that wasn't the problem. His brain was stuck in a continuous loop, just like a computer. He replayed the tragic event over and over. A computer he could fix, but his own brain was betraying him. He wished he had been asleep in his own bed when the blast occurred. He would be spared this agony.

Jake finished his devotion and shut off the light as he headed to his bed. His eyes were heavy as he pulled back the covers. It was always nice to sleep in a bed that wasn't moving down the road at seventy miles per hour. Yes, mph; he didn't care if the whole world was metric. In his mind, and on his log, everything was still in mph until he absolutely had to convert it. It was one of the only things he had anymore that he could cling to from when he actually drove his truck.

He heard the kid turn off the TV and slide into bed. Minutes later, he heard him scream and sit upright in his bed. He could see in the shadows that he had grabbed his head with both hands as his body swayed in grief. Jake remembered his own grief when a roadside bomb tore into his convoy back in Iran and killed his buddies, and again when his own son was killed. He wouldn't get much sleep tonight either.

—◊—

Morning came too early. Jake got up and dressed and headed for the bathroom. He shaved and brushed his teeth and combed what was left of his hair. He noticed David staring into space.

"Let's go down to the lobby and get some breakfast. I'll call a car, and we can eat while we wait."

"Ok."

David's mouth was thick from the night's nightmares and the fact that he hadn't brushed his teeth in over two days. He didn't have a comb or a toothbrush. He dressed and went down to the lobby and got what he needed from a vending machine, along with some headache pills for his pounding head.

After he finished, he and Jake walked down to the lobby and got in line for the continental breakfast. The car was on its way, so they sat down and ate a doughnut and drank coffee. They spotted the car and hastily got up and put their trash in the container. David also put his debris from the hair dye fiasco and the toothache stuff in the trash. It would be less likely to be discovered there than in the hotel room. They walked to the car and got in.

"Can you take me to the train station?" David asked, eyes straight ahead and his head down. If I stay with you, I could cause you a lot of grief. If the people who want me dead were willing to wipe out my whole family to get to me, then they might come after you too."

"What makes you think you haven't already caused me a lot of grief?" Jake said with a big grin on his face. "Sure, if that is what you want."

He punched in the address and the car pulled out. They rode in silence. Too soon for David, they pulled into the station. He was about to lose his second father figure in less than a week. They both got out of the car.

David stuck out his right hand, and Jake grasped it.

"Thanks for not turning me in, Jake. I'll never forget you."

"I know you won't, kid! I'm unforgettable." Jake grinned.

David appreciated the tease. The next thing he knew, he was in a bear hug so tight it squeezed a tear out of his eye.

Jake turned and got in the car to leave. The car drove away. He looked straight ahead with his head down, saying a prayer for this kid who had helped him grieve.

David walked away, thinking he would never be David to anyone ever again.

CHAPTER 7

The New Life

Elias walked to the kiosk to buy a train pass to the next destination available. It was Detroit, Michigan, good as anywhere. He swiped his bit-card and waited for the machine to spit out his ticket. He got a window seat. He had an hour to kill, so he walked around the station.

He walked into a shop that sold communications devices and computers. He'd thought about getting a new phone, but who could he call? If he tried to contact anyone from his old life, they would be able to track him. Instead, he looked at the latest computer.

He used to put together his own computers, so he knew which brands made the components he was looking for and which ones were compatible and adaptable to the newest software, not that he would buy any software, as he could produce his own. Then and only then would he know it was secure for what he had in mind.

It was a small store and didn't have what he wanted, so he went next door to a sub shop and bought a sandwich and a bottle of water to take with him. In the next shop, he bought a backpack, so he looked like the average traveler, and stuck his sandwich and water in it. He bought some new clothes and went to the restroom and put them on. He put his dirty clothes in the plastic store bag and put them in the backpack.

He hustled to the boarding area just as his train departure was announced. He felt better with the new clothes. He boarded and settled into his seat. Even on this bullet train that traveled 300 kilometers per hour, the trip would take over ten hours with the stops in Kansas City, St. Louis, and Chicago.

He thought about his future in Detroit. He wasn't sure why he chose this route. Maybe it was because the second Browning Foundation community was established there.

After years of infrastructure neglect and the decline of the American auto industry, Detroit was in default. The government had promised too much for too long, and the latest hiccup in the economy had put the city over the brink. Of course, the poor suffered the most. There had been riots in the streets when the first subsidy payments didn't arrive.

The federal government could no longer bail the city out because the feds were in default also. Foreign creditors had finally had enough of the seemingly endless and reckless spending and called in the trillions of dollars of debt owed. That opened the door for the dollar being deposed by the bitcoin as a world-recognized currency.

The United States of America, once the most powerful nation in the world, was unable to pay its bills. Once again, the noble socialist experiment had failed. When the new government took over, it promised nirvana and bliss but delivered despair and poverty. When Alonzo Browning proposed that he could reverse the slide into anarchy, the local officials were more than glad to hear him out.

His ideas were not new; the country had been founded on the very principles that he lived by. He was an extreme and very passionate capitalist. He dusted off the old Constitution of the

United States and taught the principles with a Christ-centered, ten-commandments-based philosophy. Elias sometimes, when he was young, accompanied his father on his many sermons and lectures. Alonzo railed against the socialist agenda, but he also brought the capitalists to their knees.

His favorite quote was, "CAPITALISM WITHOUT CHRIST IS JUST GREED!"

He'd been kicked out of most colleges and large venues but still he preached his message. He was a modern-day Billy Graham and Martin Luther King Jr. rolled into one. He had a large following, and when Elias agreed to fund his noble experiment, all he needed was a venue to prove his ideas.

It had worked back in Hamilton County, but that was a small-town rural area. The vast areas of Detroit that had been abandoned could be bought for fractions of the bitcoin value. It was ideal. The government needed the revenue right now, and the Browning Foundation could provide that. The foundation bought 70 of the 370 square kilometers of the inner city. Mostly it was abandoned properties with squatters (human and animal) who had to be dealt with, overgrown brush and weeds, and just general neglect.

The government publicly applauded Browning's efforts but behind closed doors the officials prepared for him to fail. After all, if he succeeded, their corrupt, flawed socialism would suffer a humiliating defeat.

Elias never got involved with the foundation. He knew of the general benefits because he had experienced the change in the place he called home. Drug use, crime, poverty, and, yes, even the misery that could be seen on every street corner in the small town near his house disappeared. He felt the need to connect with his family through their legacy. It was all he had left.

The train slowed for his last stop in Detroit. The train tracks had high, concrete barriers with razor sharp concertina wire around the top to keep out terrorists and derelicts. It went by so fast, the passengers were cautioned to not focus on the barrier. It caused some people to get vertigo. The train entered the tunnel with a shudder. The magnetic brake hummed, and Elias felt an odd sensation as the magnetism railed against the inertia and fought with the massive object to slow it safely to a stop at just the right location at the station.

He gathered his bag from under the seat and joined the mass exodus of humans into the station. He stopped abruptly and with an air of uncertainty looked around for the signs prompting passengers into whatever flocks they belonged.

Because he didn't have any luggage to claim, he chose the flock heading toward the driverless taxis and busses. Most people knew what bus to get on to get where they wanted to go. The businesspeople hailed taxis and were soon gone.

He decided not to get into the fray of all the alpha males and females competing for the next available car ride. Instead, he studied the destination board at the bus kiosk. New Detroit, that's where he wanted to go. There were three stops in New Detroit, and he didn't really know which one to choose. Because he didn't have a phone to research the information he needed, he picked up a brochure and studied it. The bus was now full, and he would have to catch the next one.

It seemed odd to be thumbing through the glossy pages of a booklet. He usually did everything on a phone or a computer screen. The last time he remembered reading a book was on his mother's lap when he was a small boy. The grief welled up in him, choking his air, while tears slid down his face. He quickly wiped the tears and read on.

"New Detroit, or Brownstown as it is fondly known by the locals, is a community founded by the vision of Alonzo Browning and funded by the Browning Foundation for the rejuvenation of the city. Come, join our efforts. All that is required is the desire to work. We offer free education, training, and above all, opportunity! Come as you are, and be transformed!"

Sounded like a cult to him, but that is where he was bound. He turned back to the brochure, and found that the second bus stop in Brownstown was in front of the registration center. That's where he needed to go. He heard the hiss of airbrakes as the next bus arrived. He thought back to Jake Tanner and his own flight of fear from his boyhood home. Melancholy gripped him as he boarded the bus. What was he doing here? He could have been a thousand kilometers from here in a beach house overlooking the ocean or in the mountains hiding from his grief in solitude, but he was drawn here. It was a feeble attempt to connect again with his father.

The bus pulled away from the curb and merged smoothly into traffic. The scene outside the bus could be from any city in the country; skyscrapers defined the horizon. As they passed through to the urban area, the scenery changed. Dilapidated houses seemed to occur more frequently. Windows were broken and boarded up or covered by ragged blankets. Doors hung precariously askew. Cars abandoned on the street seemed to have every sellable part removed. One had a stray dog squatting in it with a litter of pups. Her ribs stuck out, and she trembled as her litter suckled the life out of her. Unless her hunt was successful that night, they might all perish. Yards were overgrown and large tree limbs from past winds and winter storms lay in agony all over the ground and against houses.

The landscape abruptly changed as he saw the welcome to New Detroit sign. The houses were freshly painted, and drapes, instead of ragged blankets, hung in the windows. The lawns were manicured, and the trees were well maintained. The cars were roadworthy and actually had license plates. A curious thing though, they all seemed to be older models with steering wheels, like they were driven instead of directed. The same sunshine fell on both cities, but its reflection seemed to be brighter from the New Detroit side of the bus. The bus made its first stop in New Detroit. Elias was amazed at the difference in the tale of the two cities.

The next stop, he climbed off the bus and walked away from the crowd to the corner of the street just to observe and get a feel for this place. He noted that the flags were at half-staff. When the crowd thinned, he walked back to the entrance of the registration building. It was a Catholic church that doubled as a registration office. He walked up the steps into a foyer that had a receptionist to answer questions and direct people to their counselors at the appointed time. A real person, not a robot or an android, a real person was at the desk.

The line was long, snaking around temporary rope barriers, like at an airport. The line moved quickly as the receptionist asked if the applicant had filled out the paperwork online and what counselor was appointed to him or her. Occasionally she passed out paperwork and told the applicant to go sit at the group W bench in the next room and fill it out. She would then assign a counselor.

When Elias approached the desk, he saw a picture of his father in a frame on her desk. He couldn't help himself from touching it gently.

She caught his gesture and asked, "Did you know him?"

"Yes, but not as well as I should have."

She thought that was a strange answer but didn't comment. "He is the reason Brownstown exists," she said, and then asked, "Do you have an appointment?"

"No."

"Did you fill out the paperwork online?"

"No, I didn't."

She handed him his paperwork and motioned him to the group W bench—the will call section. He filled out the paperwork. It only took about two minutes. He waited.

"Montague?" a robust voice attached to a middle-aged man announced, looking toward the group W bench.

"Elias Montague . . . Elias Tobias Montague?"

It finally dawned on him the person was talking about him! He'd never heard it out loud. "Sorry, I was daydreaming," he excused himself as he jumped up and followed the man into a cubicle.

When inside, he sat down in the chair the man motioned toward.

"Name's Daniel DuPont," the man said as he extended his hand.

Elias jumped up and shook the man's hand and then sat back down.

The kid has good manners, DuPont thought. *I can count on one hand how many times I elicited that response.*

"What brings you to Brownstown, Mr. Montague?"

"I read one of your brochures," Elias replied. It wasn't a lie; he did read the brochures at the bus stop.

"Let me give you a rundown of what we require of you and what you can expect from us. First, you will work. There is no welfare here. We will send you to the school of your choice for free. That includes trade school, culinary school, or even advanced computer labs for IT training. We can get you a driver's license, a pilot's license, or teach you maritime skills, although they aren't much good outside Brownstown. We have one hundred percent placement, and we partner you with a mentor to ensure your success. No one plays the victim here. Your success is up to you! If you are caught with drugs of any kind, we send you to a drug rehab and start over.

"Our resources are not unlimited, so we have a three-strikes-and-you-are-out rule. Three offenses and you will be asked to leave. Drinking is permitted, but don't drive drunk. Call a self-drive if you need to sober up. We do not have liquor stores or taverns in Brownstown, but you can buy it anywhere outside in Detroit.

"We require you to go through extensive firearms training, after which you can make up your own mind if you want to carry a gun. We also have training for the latest Taser and laser weapons. There are a lot of bad people outside Brownstown who see our success and want to help themselves to it. Our police force is stretched thin, so we need the cooperation of everyone to keep the city safe. Voting is a right and a requirement. We look out for our neighbors and volunteer five hours a week. Any questions, Mr. Montague?"

Elias just shrugged and nodded no.

"I see here that you have checked that you have training in computer technology."

"Yes, I have a degree from MIT in computer science. I would like to work in that field, if possible."

"MIT! What are you doing here?"

"I am tired of the government requiring tracking software imbedded in every program I write!" Elias replied, which was the truth.

Daniel studied him for a second before he replied, trying to get a feel for this guy and wondering if he was being truthful.

"We can always use computer geeks," he finally said with a grin.

Elias hadn't heard that term for years.

"Do you need financial assistance, Elias?"

"No, I have enough to pay my way until I get established. I do need a place to stay."

Daniel was glad to hear that. Too many times the people he helped had nothing to their name but the clothes on their back. They had made so many bad decisions in life they couldn't see a way out. They came here for a fresh start. Most stayed, some didn't. Some couldn't handle the schooling, or the hard work, or the attitude of being responsible for their own actions.

"We will assign you a mentor and you can start work next Wednesday. That will give you time to settle in. You can stay in the hotel down the street until we can get an apartment ready for you. Come back Friday at eight a.m. and we'll go over your placement."

"Thanks. Is there a place nearby to buy computers?"

Yes, past the hotel about ten blocks. They are closed now, but they will open at eight tomorrow morning.'

"Ok, I'll check it out tomorrow."

Elias got up and shook Daniel's hand as he left. He wondered how much background checking was done on him as he sat in the counselor's office. The whole time he was talking, Daniel was typing on his computer. His new identity must have been good enough for this background check at least.

Elias checked into the hotel and went up to his room. After a long hot shower, he went back down through the lobby and out the front door.

The sidewalk oozed the sun's heat into the air on this hot, late August afternoon. He turned on a side street and walked until he found a small, storefront restaurant and went inside. The cool of the air conditioner hugged him with a welcome caress. The place wasn't busy, so he found his own seat and waited. A young woman, who seemed to him to be a little older than he was, came out to wait on him. She had dark hair and hazel eyes and one of those smiles that light up a room.

"I'm closed, but as you are here, what can I get for you this hot afternoon? I've got some really good vegetable soup and fresh baked peach pie. It's hard to beat peach pie with fresh Michigan peaches!"

"Sounds good, if you'll throw in sweet tea."

"Coming right up."

There was an older couple sitting across the room talking about nothing and everything, lost in their own world. As the woman brought him his order, they got up to leave. They smiled at him and waved as if they knew him. It reminded him of home. He smiled back. He sipped his tea and started in on the soup.

It was really good. The presentation was great. The crackers were set in a sunflower arrangement around the bowl with a little sprig of color. Instead of the napkin rolled around the silverware, it was placed on the table with the silverware positioned the way it should be in the old etiquette books. The woman came by after she took care of the old couple and said her goodbyes to them.

"How is everything?" she asked, while wiping down a table next to him.

"Great! You obviously enjoy what you are doing," he managed to reply between bites.

"Yes, yes, I do, very much. My husband was killed in the riots. He was just coming home from work when a rioter threw a brick and hit him in the temple. He died on the spot. I was desperate. I couldn't find work anywhere. My kids were starving, and I couldn't get welfare. The government couldn't pay the people who were already in the system and weren't taking other applicants.

"The night before we were going to be evicted, we left with what we could carry. I only had enough money to take the bus twenty-five kilometers to the edge of New Detroit. We walked the remaining ten kilometers in the dark of night to get to the registration center. I was never so scared in my life!"

He studied her as she talked. He took another bite as she went on.

"I went to culinary school. Not only did I learn to cook, the instructors taught business practices and how to run a restaurant. My mentor moved to be closer to her grandchildren and sold me this place. My boys and I live in the upstairs apartment. I vowed when I was accepted to school that my children would never go hungry again, and here we are, surrounded by food all the time! God is good!"

He finished his soup, pushed the bowl away, and pulled his pie close. She whisked the empty bowl away just as he let go of it. He watched her intently as she went into the kitchen.

He took a bite of the pie and let out an audible but involuntary, "mmmmmhhh."

Her face lit up as she walked back toward him.

"Best peach pie in the world, isn't it?"

"Yeah!" he said with his mouth full and his head tilted back so he wouldn't lose any pie as he talked, his mouth contorted.

"I'm not really open for business right now; I open early to catch the construction crowd in the morning and the businesspeople at lunch. I close officially around three, so I can be with my kids after school. Coy and Birdie, the older couple who were here, are locals who love to come in here every afternoon and just hang out together and eat a slice of pie with some coffee. Their health is failing, so I don't know how much longer they will be coming, but I'll stay open for them until they no longer can come."

"That's nice of you, going above and beyond like that," he said, then he swigged his tea.

She looked at him quizzically with her head tilted a little, "You're new here, aren't you?" she asked.

"Yeah, I just got off the bus."

"That's just what we do here. That is what sets us apart from the rest of the world. Alonzo insisted we treat others as we want to be treated."

"Mark 12:31. And the second is like, namely this, Thou shalt love thy neighbour as thyself. There is none other commandment greater than these."

She smiled that big beautiful smile with her eyes wide. "Are you a Christian?" she asked with excitement.

"Nah, I just know the Bible from cover to cover, learned it when I was a kid." He had already said too much. He was going to have to learn not to quote scripture if he didn't want to be asked that question. He finished his pie and the last of his tea.

"Would you like some more tea?"

"No, I'd better not. It will keep me up all night."

He got up to leave, not really wanting to go, but at a loss for any excuse to stay. He fumbled with his bit-card and walked over to the kiosk to pay. She followed. He caught a whiff of her

THE FINGERPRINT OF FAITH

perfume as she walked. He tried to be discreet as he breathed in as much as he dared without being obvious. He couldn't describe the feeling in his stomach.

"Well, I better be going," he said, but his legs didn't move.

"Come back again!" she said with a little more sincerity than she used for other customers.

He took that as his cue to leave and waved slightly as he ran awkwardly into the doorframe and had to back up and try again to get out. She smiled as he left, hoping she would see him again soon.

He walked on air around the corner to his hotel. He took two steps at a time as he bounded up the stairs to the room. He couldn't understand where all his energy was coming from. He was dead tired before he ate. It must be that soup. He didn't know it yet, but he was going to eat there every evening he possibly could. He got ready for bed. As he settled under the covers, he smelled her perfume again. He actually slept soundly for the first time since the tragedy.

The sun was high when he awoke. He jumped out of bed and dressed. He hurried down to the lobby and grabbed a doughnut off the almost empty tray and stuck it in his mouth as he poured a cup of coffee. He shoved a lid on the cup and hurried out the door. The doughnut was gone in three bites and he took the lid off the coffee and took a sip. It was way too hot and burned his tongue. He blew on it, as he hurried to the computer store.

He hoped he hadn't waited too long to finish morphing his identity to Elias. He had left loose ends, too many loose ends. He finished his coffee and threw the cup in the trash container by the front door to the computer store as he opened the door.

57

The guy inside smiled as he greeted him. Everybody smiled here. He managed a forced smile. His tongue hurt, and he really wasn't feeling it.

"I want to see your fastest computer with the most memory."

The guy wasn't halfway through his spiel when Elias said, "I'll take it. I'll need your best monitor and another external hard drive with the most storage. Also, do you have any of the silicon paper?"

"You mean the stuff made by Sanddollar?"

"Yeah, that's the stuff. Do you have any wire and blank circuit boards or half boards? Here's a list of all the components I'll need."

"Sure, you need liquid solder too? I got some great stuff, just put the circuit together and put a little solder on, then put it under a UV light for about thirty seconds and you're done. How about USB plugs? I have them too."

"Sure, I'll need a toolkit for working on electronic stuff."

The guy was almost salivating as he wrung up the purchases. That was more computer stuff than he sold in a week sometimes. Most of his money came from phones and gaming devices. Elias picked up his sack and the monitor and nodded to the guy as he left.

Back in his hotel room, he went about the task of setting up his new toys. He would have to make his fingerprint circuit later; right now he wanted to get the computer running. He powered it up and went about the task of writing his software.

With the speed of an android, his fingers flew over the keys. He was in a trance as he concentrated on the task at hand. He shut his eyes and visualized the code he was creating. He could see in his mind's eye the computer converting his commands to the binary off-on it used to create intelligence at a speed limited only by the silicon synopsis. He couldn't use the antiquated and unsecured Wi-Fi for what he had in mind, so he unplugged the TV and fashioned an adapter to use the cable to get to the cloud blockchain storage system he created.

It would be a while before the machine finished the creation and downloading of his software that required the Web connection, so he set about creating the fingerprint gloves that he used to make his back-door hacking system. He took the external memory drive and fashioned a control device that he could hook up to his computer through the membrane paper that he had fashioned into finger cots. Every time he connected the end of his fingers to the right key in the right sequence, he could access any system he had created. He originally invented this to protect his proprietary licenses on all his software, but the nature of the invention allowed him access to most all programs undetected. When he put on the gloves, he resembled a cyborg. He had wires dangling from his forearms that disappeared behind the computer into the makeshift circuit board plugged into one of its ports.

The computer was silent. The monitor came alive with a picture of the Grand Canyon. "WELCOME, ELIAS, WHAT WOULD YOU LIKE TO DO TODAY?" Many icons appeared on the desktop. He was back in business. He wanted to access his personal accounts and delete any information his family had stored, like pictures, stories, bank accounts, records, and any links to David Browning. He typed in his passwords, and then downloaded and deleted all the information in the cloud. He would sort it out later. Right now, he just needed to secure the family history.

He opened another site that stored his personal security camera pictures. He would sort through everything tomorrow. He had been at this all day without stopping, and he was hungry. He thought of the woman in the café down the street. Funny, he didn't used to let a little thing like hunger stop him from his computer quests.

He jumped in the shower. When he got out, he realized he only had the clothes he had on from that day and the clothes he escaped in. They were both dirty. He'd never given a second thought to his appearance before.

He would ask in the lobby if there was a store around that sold men's clothing. He combed his hair and put on some deodorant, then combed his hair again. He got dressed and headed for the lobby. The staff member directed him to a store about ten blocks in the opposite direction he really wanted to go. Because he didn't have a phone, he couldn't call a self-drive. He started toward the clothing store at a fast walk. He was lost in thought and almost walked past the store. It occurred to him that he hadn't seen a big box store or a large chain store of any kind since he'd arrived in Brownstown. He'd ask the woman at the diner why that was, if he remembered.

He entered the clothing store, thankful for the air conditioning. He was browsing when a well-dressed guy came up to him and asked if he needed help.

"Yeah," he replied, "I'm looking for a couple of sets of clothes that are easy to wash and wear and not too expensive."

"Come with me. I've got just what you are looking for."

Elias followed him to the back section of the store. He looked for his size on the many racks and various styles of shirts and pants.

"Casual or office dress or work clothes?" the clerk asked.

Elias noticed the big smile on the guy's face. It seemed like everyone had a joy about them that he couldn't ignore.

"Casual," he replied, looking around at the intimidating array.

The guy pulled out some colors that Elias liked and in his size too. He headed to the dressing room and tried them on, along with some dress jeans. They fit him well, so he left one pair on and told the guy he'd take everything. He gathered all the clothes and headed to the checkout.

"How'd you know my size?" Elias wondered.

"It's what I get paid for," the guy grinned. He was appreciative of the recognition.

Elias paid for the merchandise and left. The clerk waved and smiled again. The shadows were getting long when he exited the store. He walked as fast as he could toward his hotel, bounded up the steps to his room, swiped his key card, opened the door, and threw his packages on the bed. Then he shut the door and hurried out.

As he hurried to the diner, he hoped Coy and Birdie hadn't left yet. As he neared the entrance, they opened the door to leave. They recognized him and waved as they walked to their house just down the street. He bounded in the door and hurried to his table and slid in, all in one motion. He was breathing a little hard as he settled in.

The woman saw him from the checkout and smiled. She had been checking the door every so often, hoping he would show.

"Is it too late to get served?" he asked, trying to keep the pleading from creeping in to his voice.

"No, I'm still unofficially open," she said with that beautiful smile.

"What's on the menu tonight?" he smiled back. He couldn't help himself. "I'm going to need more than soup tonight, I'm starved!"

"How about a T-bone steak with baked potato, loaded with sour cream and chives, with a side of steamed broccoli covered in cheese? I still have one piece of peach pie left."

"Yes, ma'am! I could go for that, medium on the steak."

She smiled and left to prepare the order. He could hear her singing in the kitchen, cooking and singing in sync, pure joy emanating from every note. He sat in silence, his ears drinking in every note as the smell of his dinner wafted through the dining area. He didn't even know her name, but he was smitten.

In a short time, she brought out his dinner. Because Coy and Birdie had already left, he had her undivided attention. She brought everything in one trip on a large tray that was used to save steps. He noticed the sweet tea on the tray and smiled at the fact that she remembered. She slid into the booth on the other side and stuck out her hand.

"Name's Abigail Vandevender."

"Elias Tobias Montague," he managed to stutter, as he shook her hand and looked briefly into her eyes.

Her hand was soft, but there was an underlying strength to her handshake. He didn't want to let go. It was the first he had experienced anything like this, and he didn't want the moment to end.

"People call me Abby for short."

"Elias," he muttered as he reluctantly let go.

When he stood to shake her hand, he lost his napkin under the table and spilled some of his tea when his legs shook the table. He sheepishly sat back down and retrieved his napkin and arranged his plate and his drink in preparation to eat.

"Where you from, Elias Tobias?" she asked as she was wiping up the tea. She liked the way the name rolled off her tongue.

"Albuquerque, New Mexico, is where I left, but I was born in Ames, Iowa.

She loved to watch people enjoy her cooking, but especially him. For some reason, she was drawn to him. She hadn't felt these feelings since her husband passed. It was time for her to move on. He seemed to relish every bite of the food.

"I'm going to check on my boys. I'll be right back."

He was starved, but he ate slowly, hoping she would return soon. He was sipping his tea when she reappeared. That smile reassured him that all was right with the kids.

"They're doing homework. I have to keep after them to finish before they can play games. They try to con me sometimes, but my mom senses kick in, and I usually am able to keep them in check." She wondered how he felt about her being a mom.

"Yeah, I can remember my mom doing the same thing," he chuckled, and then he squelched the grief and swallowed hard when the memory intruded on his brain.

"My mom is still living in Toledo, but Dad died five years ago," she volunteered, wanting him to share the same information.

When he didn't, she just flat-out asked, "What about yours?"

"They're dead," he said matter-of-factly. His mood darkened, and he changed the subject, "This pie is the best."

"Thank you."

The conversation lagged, so she picked up the dishes and took them to the kitchen. She wasn't smiling when she returned. She knew she had hit a nerve and was sorry she ever brought it up. She sat back down, but the awkward silence continued. He so wanted to see that smile. He needed to see that smile. He racked his brain to think of something to ask her that would get the conversation going again.

"Uhh," they both said in unison.

"You go," she said.

"I was just going to ask you about your boys."

Her face lit up again, and the smile was back. She started to talk about her children. She talked and talked. He was glad to have the excuse to study her face and look into her eyes. He nodded occasionally, but he was lost in her and had to fight to listen to what she was saying.

"And that's about it."

He was caught gazing into her eyes.

"I can tell you're really proud of those kids," he stammered, recovering the moment.

Her smile was back. They talked about everything and nothing. Two hours they talked. Abby finally brought them back from the future when she glanced at her watch and jumped up.

"I'm sorry! I have to get the kids to bed. I didn't realize it was so late!"

She walked over to the bit-card reader. He reluctantly followed. As he was paying for the meal, she asked, "Have you found a church anywhere?"

"No."

"I go to the Christian church about ten blocks south of here. I'd really like for you to attend. We are going to have a special service on Sunday honoring Alonzo Browning, the founder of New Detroit."

In reality, he hadn't been to church since he turned eighteen, and his parents told him it was his decision. At the time, it seemed so liberating to not have to be bothered. Now, though, he'd do anything to be with her.

"I'll have to think about it, I wouldn't know anyone."

"You'd know me. Tomorrow is Friday, and I'm not here Saturday at this time of day, so you can let me know what you think tomorrow. That is, if you'll be back tomorrow." She realized she was assuming a lot and was a little embarrassed.

"Yeah, I'll let you know tomorrow."

He smiled and waved as he opened the door to leave. He watched her tidy up through the plate glass window as he walked away. It was nearly dark.

—ɯ—

The next morning, he woke with a scream, his bed drenched in sweat. He got out of bed and splashed water on his face. He looked in the mirror at his face. He didn't know the guy staring back anymore. He had bags under his eyes, and his skin was creased with stress lines that made him look twice his age. He couldn't see what Abby saw in him, if anything. Maybe she was just this nice to everyone.

Depression settled on him like heavy dew on an Indiana summer night. It wasn't daylight yet, but he knew he couldn't spend another second in that bed. He got up and went in the bathroom to turn on the shower. He stepped in and let the hot water cascade over his body. He leaned his forehead on the wall under the showerhead and cried like a baby. How he wished he could feel his mother's touch and hear her voice.

When the hot water had washed away all the dew it could, he got out and toweled off. He didn't think he could handle the tribute Sunday, no matter how bad he wanted to be with Abby. He dressed and went to the lobby to see if there was any coffee or doughnuts out yet.

He remembered he had to meet with Daniel this morning to confirm his placement and find out the progress Daniel had made on finding him an apartment. The staff were just setting up the breakfast when he walked into the room. He leisurely browsed the selection and poured a cup of coffee and some orange juice. He found a seat next to the window looking onto the street and placed his selections on the table.

He watched taxis pick up the businesspeople on a quest for more. An elderly couple got in a taxi slowly, unsteady on their feet. The look of concern on their faces made him wonder if they were heading to a hospital or a clinic for treatment of an incurable disease that would separate them after all the years they had had together. He was morose like that when he was down. He tended to imagine the worse. He ate slowly and watched the sun's rays paint a portrait on the blank canvas that would be Friday.

At eight o'clock, he was sitting in the registration center waiting for Daniel. He rose from the group W bench when he spotted Daniel coming in the door. He stuck out his hand when he approached.

"Elias Montague, I'm your first appointment today."

"Oh, yes," he said, shifting his coffee cup to his left hand, so he could shake Elias's hand. He sipped coffee as he opened the door and went in to start his day. There were already many people lining up in the foyer. Elias followed Daniel and watched him as he hit the keys to wake his computer for the day.

It stretched and yawned as the screen came to life. Daniel set his coffee cup on an empty space on his desk and, still standing, tapped on the keyboard until Elias's folder appeared. While the machine was gathering the information it was commanded to, Daniel pulled up his chair, sipped more coffee, and got comfortable. As soon as the computer binary symphony ended, Daniel looked up at Elias.

"We've got you in the Gatewood complex, first building to the left, apartment twenty-nine. I'll print the directions along with your lease. Just show the lease to the office and the manager will take care of setting up your rent payments. The unit has been totally renovated and furnished. You'll need personal items, kitchen utensils, and linens, that kind of thing, but everything else is there. You can move in Monday. We also have you set up with a new startup called Envirowheels. It takes all the old cars, whether abandoned or turned in on trade, and installs the latest drive systems in them. The cars sell at a fraction of what a new self-drive goes for. The company also sell software and sensors for self-drives to the auto industry. Their problem is the computer management systems are giving them fits. They need a good team of IT experts to bail them out. We've assigned Darious as your mentor. You start Wednesday."

He got up as soon as the printer was finished and handed the packet to Elias.

"This is a new start, son, don't mess it up. You didn't raise any red flags when we checked you out, so I'm expecting big things from you."

Elias thought this spiel could have been right out of his father's repertoire. He got up to leave. He extended his hand to Daniel, and they shook. Daniel had developed a good judge of character, and there wasn't a doubt in his mind this kid would make it.

CHAPTER 8

Walking in a Cloud

Elias walked back to his hotel room. He had a lot of investigating, or hacking, to do, depending on whose point of view. He threw the packet on the bed; he'd deal with it later. He turned on the computer and booted it up to check on his status, or rather the status of David Browning. He donned his cyborg gloves and started his quest for answers. First, he hacked into his cameras back home. He typed the codes without thinking. They were a part of his brain, just like the Bible was. He didn't have time to watch the videos now, so he created a file to check them later and send them, if necessary.

He typed slowly and precisely. He was entering the blockchain world of cloud storage technology. He had to walk softly and carefully, so he wouldn't be detected. First, he checked the Rothfellas' new technology for weaknesses. He stroked the keys like a pianist lost in a concerto. Even with the fastest computer, this was going to take time. He followed threads that led nowhere. He floated on the wave of information flowing in the binary ocean, bobbing up and down, checking every fickle lead until he found an obscure thread of information in a dark and hidden part of their cloud.

Lots of wealth hovered around this ominous place. He knew he couldn't attempt to download anything for fear of being detected. He made a mental note of the path that had gotten him in this part of the blockchain. He knew it would take him many trips to sort out the information he was looking for. Methodically, carefully, he followed the delicate thread he had imbedded in the blockchain cloud.

He was getting tired. Fatigue can lead to mistakes, so he exited the cloud and opened the folder that contained his security camera data. He poured over the cameras. Mostly, he saw the comings and goings of squirrels and coons. The neighbor's cat made frequent forays into the yard to hunt and leave her calling card. He forwarded the file to three in the morning. He saw himself quietly slip out the back door and into the woods. He concentrated on the cameras aimed at the front of the property and those aimed at his bedroom.

At three-fifteen, a large drone could be seen approaching the front of the property. As it came into the camera's view, it positioned itself for a split second before unleashing the biggest ball of compressed hydrogen particle energy he'd ever seen. It was right out of a science fiction movie. There were rumors of the development of such weapons. They resembled the energy of the sun, only the hydrogen was forced under tremendous pressure into an unstable molecular structure such as nitroglycerin at temperatures approaching absolute zero. A laser was used to detonate the device nanoseconds after it reached its target. The laser raised the core temperature of the bomb past its critical temperature. The resulting explosion created an intense blast. The hydrogen burned all the oxygen in the air. The percussion and intense heat killed every living thing. The bomb exploded with such intensity that all traces of it were vaporized. There was no chemical residue, no fire, no evidence, and no survivors.

Whoever was behind this wanted to make a statement, or maybe they were just inept and poorly trained. Whatever the reason, his family was dead and the only place he ever called home was destroyed. He poured over the footage, frame by frame, trying to get some kind of identifying marks on the drone.

He'd had enough of the morbid footage. He had to get out of his room and get some air. The rage he felt was indescribable. He burst out of the hotel lobby at a dead run. He ran until his lungs ached and his legs trembled. He bent over with his hands on his knees like the night he became a fugitive. The rage was slowly dissipating with every breath. It was replaced by remorse. Why had he gone into the woods at that particular time? Why were they, the innocents, killed, and why was he spared? He stumbled onto a small, park bench and sat down with his head in his hands and started to rock back and forth with grief.

For the first time in a long time, he prayed. He prayed angry prayers demanding to know why he was still here on earth when his family had perished. He prayed prayers of anguish. He prayed prayers demanding to know what he had done to deserve this. He prayed until he was mentally exhausted. When he finished, he felt emptiness all the way to his soul. He started to walk back to his room. Every step was agony. When he thought he had reached his limit of endurance, a still, small voice form within urged him on.

"You must continue to carry on. You must continue to carry on. You . . . must continue to . . . carry on!" the voice urged from within.

After an eternity, in his mind, he found himself climbing the steps to his hotel room. He struggled with the lock and stumbled inside. He crawled into bed and lay in a fetal position in his clothes. The night noises faded into a stupor.

—⁊⁊⁊—

Abby waited in anticipation for him to show. She had even baked another pie. He seemed to enjoy it so much. Coy and Birdie had been gone for an hour and still she was pretending to tidy up, hoping he would come through the door, famished. She turned out the lights and went up to get her children ready for bed. She was glad Saturday was a short workday. She didn't sleep well.

—⁊⁊⁊—

He rose in the predawn hour once again. Sleep would not come. He returned to his computer like an addict to his drug. He donned his cyborg hands and entered the altered reality of the blockchain cloud, looking for more answers. He hacked into the database for the Ultimate Security cameras hoping to see something that his cameras had missed. He downloaded the data for the same time as his cameras. He pored over the files in the early morning, following the same protocol that he used with his own data. When he got to the front cameras that should have picked up the drone's presence, there was no data recorded.

It dawned on him that the detectives would be seeing the same thing. He hacked into the Hamilton County sheriff's office and the state police office until he found the case files for criminal investigation. The detectives, Dan Bolker and Justin Peters, came up as the detectives in charge of the case. They were going to receive a surprise on their computers from the same thread he had used to retrieve the data from his cameras. He was careful not to let them know where it originated, so they couldn't track him.

The first rays of sunrise were intruding in his space as he sent the files. He sat at the computer for a second after sending the detectives the new information. He felt lightness in his soul. It seemed to be therapeutic to contribute something to the possibility of finding the truth in his family's deaths. He suddenly realized he was famished. He wondered if Abby's Place would be open. He walked past the continental breakfast in the hotel lobby and down the sidewalk, hoping to get some real food.

As he approached the restaurant, the fatigue lightened. He saw someone leave, so he knew she would be there preparing her unique form of art that left the diner with not only a full stomach but a light spirit. What did the Southerners call it? Soul food, or something like that?

He opened the door to the smell of the morning fare caressing his nostrils. There was the clink of glasses and the occasional sound of a fork hitting a plate. A din of conversation and the occasional laugh wafted through the air along with the aroma of the food. He waited to be seated as the place was almost full.

The waitress smiled at him as she asked, "One?"

He nodded and asked on the way to the table, "Is Abby here?"

"Darlin', Abby is always here! This place needs Abby like the flowers need rain!"

His mouth turned up in a suppressed smile. He followed her to a table for two. He sat so he could see the general direction of the kitchen.

"Coffee?" the waitress asked as she handed him a menu.

"Yes, please."

"I'll bring that out and come back for your order."

He hadn't taken his eyes off the hallway leading to the kitchen since he sat down. The waitress brought his coffee. He hadn't bothered to open the menu.

"What can I get for you?"

He didn't want her to know he didn't have a clue, so he asked, "What's the special today?"

She pointed to a menu posted above the counter on the opposite wall. He hadn't noticed.

"I'll have that," he said, still looking toward the kitchen.

The barrage of questions started. "How do you want your eggs?"

"Over easy."

"Bacon or sausage?"

"Sausage."

"White, wheat, or rye toast?"

"Wheat."

He was trying to pay attention to her, but he was too distracted. When the inquisition ended he spoke up, "Hey, would you give Abby a message for me?"

The waitress hesitated for a minute, thinking about how many guys had hit on Abby since she started working here. She was very protective of Abby. She was family, just like everyone in this place. She looked the guy over and decided she would say something as long as it didn't involve addresses or phone numbers.

"Maybe, what is it?"

"Just say Elias Tobias says hi."

She hit the appropriate key on her pad to send the order.

"You know; I don't have a place on my pad that says, 'Hi, Abby.' If I get time I'll tell her."

She went to her next table. He sipped his coffee. He thought about getting up and going back to the kitchen, but in his position he didn't want to cause a scene.

Minutes later, the waitress's pad vibrated, telling her she had an order up. She went to retrieve it and for some reason remembered what the guy requested.

"Hey, Abby, there's a guy out here who says to tell you, "Elias Tobias says hi.""

The waitress grabbed the food without hesitating and left. A smile crept onto Abby's face. The one he so craved. She wiped her hands on her apron out of habit and sneaked a peek out the pickup window. She could see him as the waitress delivered his food.

She couldn't leave yet, but the morning rush was about over. Maybe she could steal some time to say hi to him before he left. She was always the epitome of efficiency, but she seemed to fly around her kitchen as order after order left for the dining room.

The last order was filled in record time. She took a deep breath as she hesitated at the door. She swung it open with her hip and headed for the dining area.

He had picked at his food until it was cold. He was on his third cup of coffee. He had just tipped the cup when he caught sight of the smile he had been craving. He gulped the coffee and set the cup down, trying hard not to choke. He tried to compose himself when she approached. His face lit up in a broad smile of his own.

"Hi!" he tried to curb his delight but wasn't having much luck.

"Hi," she said. "Missed you last night."

"Sorry, I wasn't up to eating, just didn't feel well. Say, what time is your church tomorrow?"

"I usually leave here about nine. When the weather's nice, the boys and I walk."

"If it's ok, I'd like to tag along."

She couldn't hide her delight and that smile lit up his life again. "I'd like that. See you then!"

She couldn't afford any more time away from the kitchen, so she turned and cocked her head, batted her eyes, and flashed a smile in that way women do when they want to melt the male heart to mush. He didn't stand a chance!

She breezed through the rest of the day. She was thinking of what dress she would wear tomorrow, what lipstick shade would go well with the dress, how she would wear her hair, and myriad other things men don't realize it takes to get ready to go to church. She grinned!

He finished his now-cold breakfast and paid his bill. The waitress got a very nice tip. He floated back to his hotel room and sat down at his computer. He did more research in the cloud. The more he explored, the more he was convinced that the Rothfellas were behind his family's death. He was formulating his vengeance in his mind. He hadn't seen the smoking gun, but there was a lot of circumstantial evidence. They financed the development of the weapon used, they hired their own freelance test company, and they had access to the prototypes.

CHAPTER 9

Camera Clues

Dan Bolker and Justin Peters were going through the Monday morning ritual. It was Peter's turn to make coffee, so he was busy with that task when Bolker arrived with the doughnuts. He set them on the desk and went about settling in for the Monday morning computer work. He had to admit that this new system that coordinated all departments and put all the boring and mundane facts about every case in the database was great. It freed him and Peters to do the real detective work.

Peters walked in with a cup of coffee for him and set it on the desk. He took a bite of his favorite, jelly-filled doughnut and was about ready to take his first tentative sip of coffee when something caught his eye on the computer screen. He stopped mid-sip.

"Hey, Peters, you have to see this!"

Peters brought his coffee cup with him. This time of morning, it didn't leave his hand until the first cup was gone. He peered at the screen.

"That's the Browning house, isn't it?"

"Yeah, but it's not the same camera angles we've seen."

They both studied the screen intently. When it came around to the front of the house, the drone was clearly visible. They both watched intently as the drone unleashed a ball of energy that penetrated the front window, followed by the flash of a laser. The drone accelerated vertically at an incredible rate of speed. The house belched and exploded with such force that the cameras shuddered in the hurricane-force winds created by the destruction. The tree limbs the cameras were obviously mounted on swayed violently for a few seconds, raining leaves and small limbs everywhere. They watched over and over again. Bolker finally shut it off, and they sat in silence trying to digest what they had just witnessed.

"Where did that come from?" asked Peters. He couldn't contain his excitement.

"I don't know. We need to contact Ultimate Security and Alvin Hinn to see if he had some different cameras that he didn't tell us about the first time."

"I agree," said Peters as he picked up the phone.

Bolker called his friend, Bob Turin, at the fire department. They exchanged pleasantries and then Bolker flat-out asked him.

"Bob, would it be possible to get a boom truck out at the Browning place? We just got a bunch of videos from some phantom cameras, and we want to verify that they are really on the premises and this isn't some kind of hoax."

"Sure, is this something I need to document or is this off the record?" said the voice on the other side of the phone.

"Call it a training exercise or something. I'd rather have it off the record. How about three o'clock?"

"Ok, see you then. I'll come alone."

Bolker had a feeling, just a sixth-sense kind of feeling. The FBI had been calling and fishing for information on the case, but he was reluctant to give them anything. Frankly, there wasn't anything to give them until now. They used to cooperate fully with the feds, but after this last political shakeup they were heavy-handed and downright nasty.

"Hey, Bolker, get this! The tech that Hinn was supposed to call us back about who checked the cameras at the Browning place was found floating in Morse Reservoir this morning. His truck was found abandoned nearby. Guess we have another crime scene to go to. They are dusting for prints now and checking his log to see if they can verify when he was at the Browning house last week."

The two men picked up their gear and headed out.

"Go get the car ready, Peters. I've got something to do."

When Peters left, Bolker opened a desk drawer and pulled out an old memory stick. He plugged it into the side of his computer and downloaded the file with the camera pictures. When he was sure the download was successful, he deleted the file on his computer. He didn't want the file in the cloud or in the blockchain or anywhere that anyone could see it. He knew anyone could retrieve it if they wanted to, but because there was already a file on the cameras maybe they wouldn't think to look. It would buy him some time. When he climbed into the car, Peters was verifying the location. As soon as the door was closed, the car took off.

"When we get done at this crime scene, we need to go to the Browning place. I called Bob Turin, and he is going to bring a boom truck, so we can look for cameras in what's left of the trees around the property. We can verify by serial numbers whether the cameras belong to Ultimate Security or not. I want to make sure someone isn't pulling our chain for their fifteen minutes of fame before I make a big deal out of these new camera files."

"Good idea," Peters replied absently. He was thinking of the new scene and how the death of this guy tied in with the Browning tragedy. At least they could account for the real tech who checked the cameras. The second tech was still a mystery.

When they arrived, they interviewed the homeowner who found the body. It was face down, floating in shallow water by his boat dock. The current had pushed the body next to his boat. He was strolling down to the dock with his morning coffee to check on his boat and ready his fishing tackle for his morning trip when he felt the body slapping the side of the boat.

"When's the last time you used the boat?" Bolker asked.

"About two days ago."

"The winds and the currents, which way do they travel here?"

"We get a lot of debris floating up in this cove this time of year."

"So, the body could have been out in the lake somewhere and still ended up here?"

"Yep, it sure could."

"Did anything out of the ordinary happen around here in the last couple of days?"

"Nope, if anyone or anything comes on any of the properties around here my dog, Rufus, starts in barking, and all the other dogs in the neighborhood join him. Squirrels drive us crazy in the spring, but I'd rather know what is going on. I've got some security cameras, if you're interested in the data. I can get it for you right here on my phone."

"That's great! We'll get a tech to retrieve it for us."

They poked around the yard and the boat dock, looking for anything out of the ordinary but found nothing. The coroner was done, and the body was transported to the morgue for an autopsy.

"Hey, Don, how's things?" Bolker said as they shook hands.

"They'd be a lot better if I hadn't been called out here at the crack of dawn on a Monday morning! You guys come rolling in here at nine-thirty and expect miracles! You got it so easy!" Don rattled right back at them.

"So, what's the story on the stiff?"

"I've been here four hours working my butt off and you want me to solve the case for you, so you can spend the rest of the afternoon at Syd's drinking beer?"

"Yes, sir, you got it!"

Most cases were solved on the information Don gleaned.

"No outward marks, but he does have a broken neck. Not much bruising or contusions, but I'll get a better feel when I get him cleaned up and the autopsy done. You know the deal, toxicology screen and bloodwork in two weeks."

"Yeah, give me a call as soon as you know."

"As always."

Bolker and Peters mulled around, talking to the techs and poking around the scene as they usually did. Their routine was more for getting a feel for the crime scene than recording anything. The techs would do that. This particular scene was probably where the body ended up, not where the death occurred, so they didn't spend much time. It was getting toward lunchtime.

"Let's grab a burger at the DQ; my belly's growling," grumbled Peters.

"Sounds good."

When they got the orders at the DQ, they found a booth and slid in to eat.

"I have to tell you."

"What do you have to tell me?" asked Peters after a bite of a too-hot French fry. He let the food cool as he listened.

"I deleted the camera files from my computer. I copied them on one of the old memory sticks I keep in my desk, so don't get bent out of shape if you can't find them in the Browning file."

Peter's face had the look. He wasn't sure why his partner was being so clandestine about that file, but he trusted his instincts. He'd seen similar epiphanies play out in the past.

"What's up?" he took a bite of now-cooled fries.

"Captain says the FBI has been sniffing around the Browning file from day one. I wasn't too worried before because we didn't have anything, but this camera business might change that. That's why we're meeting Bob in a few minutes at the Browning place to check things out."

They ate in silence, each lost in thought, running different scenarios, circumstances, and what-ifs through their brains, wondering. Peters finished his last bite and abruptly got up and gathered his trash along with Bolker's. Bolker stuffed the remaining bite of food in his mouth.

They got in the car and slammed the doors simultaneously. The car drove to the Browning estate five kilometers away. As they approached the property, they noticed the trees. They looked as if a giant hand had stripped off the small limbs and the leaves. The limbs were lying on the ground helter-skelter, like a tornado had gone through.

They got out of the car and walked around gingerly with their trained eyes, searching for truth. The withered debris had already succumbed to the hot and dry August weather, it crunched under their feet like late fall foliage. They peered at the trees trying to remember the angle of the lenses as they watched the events in their mind's eyes over and over again, just like earlier in the day on the computer. Bob Turin pulled up in his boom truck.

It wasn't a big truck like found in the big cities, after all there were no skyscrapers in his jurisdiction, but he had a small stripe painted on the side of the bucket for every time a soul was saved from a fire or some other tragedy that unfolded higher than a ladder could safely reach.

He got out of the truck and walked over to the two men who were talking beside what was left of a giant oak. He still got a queasy stomach remembering a few short days ago and just how fragile life really was.

"What's the plan, Dan?" he interrupted the conversation.

They all smiled and shook hands.

Dan spoke, "I'm going to let you in on something that only we need to know." He took his hand and gestured in a circle, encompassing the three of them. "Peters and I got this video file attached to our Browning file out of the blue. It was the camera data from the night we all remember. It showed a lot more detail than the 'official' cameras from the security place. We're trying to locate the cameras that were used on the videos. I've done some homework on this kid, David. He's capable of almost anything involving electronics or computers, so I think it's possible he sent the video. We just need a camera or two to verify. We have a list of the serial numbers for the security cameras. We need to find the one that doesn't match."

"Ok, let's get to it. This tree looks like as good a place to start as any." Bob said out loud as he walked back to the truck.

He positioned the truck and got into the gondola and strapped on his harness. The two detectives pointed out where they thought a camera should be. Bob checked the bark for anything abnormal. He methodically, painstakingly moved the bucket just a bit at a time while he searched limbs facing where the house used to be. He was looking and feeling his way along the tree.

The two detectives could only wait and fidget.

Bob was about to move on when his finger felt something different on the bark. As beat up as the tree was, he didn't get his hopes up but still got a toolkit out of his vest pocket. He had a pair of magnifying lenses that looked like clown glasses and a pick that resembled a dentist tool.

He took out his multipurpose knife he always carried in his pocket and dug around the slightly raised area and used the pick to clean away the bark. He repeated the process until the tiny camera was exposed. It had been drilled into the tree, but over the course of the seasons the tree had all but encapsulated everything but the lens.

The detectives scoped out other possible locations on some of the remaining trees around the sides and the back of the house. When they walked back to Bob's location, they noticed him working on the tree.

"You find something?" Bolker asked

"Yep," Bob didn't look up; he kept on picking away at the wood. "Too bad this couldn't be a pine instead of an oak. This wood is hard."

When he finally freed the camera, he brought the bucket down as low as it would go and handed the camera to Peters.

"You are going to need these to find any ID numbers on anything that small," Bob said as he handed the glasses to Peters.

"Where to now, Bolker?

"Over here, the branch on this maple looks to be about the right camera angle."

Bob repositioned the bucket and started searching the maple tree. As before, he searched with his eyes and his hands for about a half hour when he saw it.

"Hey, Peters! Are you done with those glasses? I found another one."

"Don't bother, Bob; we're convinced that the data is for real," Peters replied.

Peters walked over from the car carrying the tiny camera. "This doesn't have any manufacturing markings on it at all. I'd bet the kid made it himself. You know as well as I do that the video file came from David," he said as he handed the camera to Bolker.

"I figured as much, but now we know," Bolker replied as he took the object and examined it. "At least we know that he is still alive."

Bob moved the boom back into position, so the truck would be roadworthy, and climbed down out of the bucket. His shirt was wet from the humid heat.

"Hope that this little thing is what you are looking for. I have to get this truck back to station number three before someone gets their nose out of joint."

"Thanks, Bob. This confirms the data is real. Don't let anyone in on this little adventure if you can help it."

Bob waved as he climbed into the truck and shut the door. The air conditioning engulfed him as he breathed in. He punched in home on the screen and the truck pulled away. He was glad to help in any way he could if it would solve this case.

The two detectives milled around at the site for a while longer, hoping some tidbit of information would be revealed. It had just been a few days since the incident, but the site seemed peaceful in the hot afternoon, like walking through a graveyard. They walked back to the car.

"We need to keep this under the radar," Bolker blurted out. "I don't know why but since the first time I set foot on that crime scene I've had an uneasy feeling that something wasn't right. This latest deal with the cameras just made it worse."

"Yeah, I wonder how the kid is doing and how he breached all the security to get this stuff to us."

They rode in silence. When they got to the station, they improvised the daily report and headed home.

The daily grind of paperwork and caseloads stretched into two weeks. Other cases occupied their workdays while they waited for the info on the alleged drowning of the security tech. There were no more surprises in the Browning files, even though they checked daily. Then Bolker's phone rang.

"Detective Bolker. Hey, how you doing, Don? Yeah, we could come down but why don't you just send the stuff . . . Oh, ok. We'll be right there."

"What's up?" asked Peters.

"That was Don Hinders. He's got the file on that drowning victim who was Ultimate Security's tech. He's sending the report through channels, but he wants to talk to us personally. I told him we'd be right there."

Peters closed out his workload on the computer and followed Bolker out the door. They were both curious why Don wanted to talk to them and glad for the chance to get out from behind the desk. The car took them in silence as they speculated and formed many scenarios in their heads.

They pulled up to the hospital and parked around the back, close to the morgue entrance and Don's office. The place was always like a walk-in freezer, but it really seemed extra cold after the hot, sunny day. Don got up to greet them as they walked in his door. His job was also fifteen minutes of excitement followed by two hours of paperwork. Peters wondered if that had something to do with his request for the meeting.

"Welcome to my digs." Don always had a hint of morgue humor. "How you guys been?"

"Great," they said almost in unison.

"What have you got that couldn't be done over the link?" Bolker followed up.

"As usual, I solved your case for you," Don volunteered, with his usual twinkle in the eye. "You two esteemed public servants just sit back and let me try to explain my findings. I have some gray areas and some theories that the official report can't convey."

"Ok, let's hear it," Bolker said as he settled in for the duration.

"The unfortunate's name is Edward Niles and he was indeed the service tech you and Ultimate Security were looking for. He was based out of and lived in Indianapolis. I told you I thought he had a broken neck on the day I was first introduced to him. was right, as usual."

Bolker rolled his eyes and grinned. At least Don's reports were never boring. He and Peters took notes as Don continued.

"There was no lake water in his lungs, so he was dead before he ended up in the water. Bruising was minimal except for normal postmortem blood pooling from the rough ride in the water and his journey through the channel to his final destination. There were no signs of struggle, so he probably was assaulted from behind. I have a theory on how his neck got broken, and that's the main reason I called you over here. There is a small, palm-sized bruise on the left side of his neck, right behind the ear next to his jaw.

"A trained killer, such as black ops, Rangers, or SEALs did this. A quick pressure and a coordinated snap of the neck lift the head at an angle that dislocates the head from the body and death is instant. With no more damage than there was to the body, I think he was rolled out of a small boat into the lake probably sometime Friday night. No blood, no ballistics, no muss, no fuss, very efficient. Of course, it's now up to you to prove what I just told you. Hey, I've done all the hard work! Here's my unofficial copy of the report for your eyes only. I don't think all my theories will fly with the brass, so I wanted you to have this one-of-a-kind autographed copy. Have at it, gentlemen!"

They sat thumbing through the report in silence until Don couldn't stand it.

"Well?" he demanded.

They both got up and shook his hand as they left.

"Nice job, Don. We'll take it from here," Peters offered as he was going out the door. "Beer at Syd's when we can get together."

"Yeah, you're buying." Don waved as they left, and he straightened his notes by tapping them on his desk.

When the two detectives arrived back at the office, they looked up the official document that Don had sent the department. It was almost as detailed as he had offered them except for the killer part. That was a lot of speculation on his part about the military-trained killer. He stated how the man died with no speculation as to who was to blame. He just wanted the two detectives to know his opinion. They were grateful for the information. They spent the rest of the day posting the files and creating a new file for Edward Niles. Peters was in charge of that today. It was his turn. It was always sad to have to put someone in the system, because it meant they had met an untimely death. It was like writing an obituary. He made sure to post a link to the Browning case.

Their shift was about over. Bolker hadn't said a dozen words all afternoon. He set about the task of duplicating the files for the Browning case and the Niles case. He would take them home and start his own case files. This was totally against the department policy, and usually his policy, but he still had a nagging feeling. If he was wrong, he could destroy the files later, but if he was right, the case wouldn't get lost in the politics that ran everyone's life today. He didn't tell Peters. If he went down for it, he didn't want to take Peters with him. He was ready for five o'clock.

The next morning, they started their routine as they normally did. The coffee was ready, and the doughnuts arrived. They were just settling in when the captain called them in—not an unusual occurrence. They briefed him frequently on all the different cases. He seemed agitated as he greeted them. He didn't go for the usual small talk.

"I just got off the phone with the FBI, and we've been ordered to turn the Browning case over under the guise of possible terrorist involvement. Send along any related files. That would also include the Niles file."

Bolker looked over at Peters with just a hint of "I told you so" in his eyes. Peters was livid. He started in on a tirade of expletives and gestures that mirrored the anger they were all feeling.

"Calm down, Peters," Bolker soothed after he thought it safe enough to intervene. His partner was pacing back and forth in his superior's office like a tormented tiger. His jugular vein in his neck had popped out, and his face was a dangerous shade of red. Bolker ushered him out of the captain's office before he said something that would leave them both in hot water.

"Come on, Peters, we're going to Syd's."

Bolker could still feel the heat of his anger as they walked to the car. It would be an early lunch, but they both had to get away for a few minutes to regroup. When they were seated, Bolker started working on his partner.

"Remember when I told you about the memory stick and the fact that I put the camera files on it? Well, I not only put the camera stuff, but the whole file for both Niles and Browning on it. I just knew by the method the house was destroyed that this could happen. We will give the official files to the feds but we won't abandon the investigation."

Peters seemed to be calming. "Why didn't you tell me?"

"I could lose my job and my pension and pretty much everything for this. I didn't want to take you down with me."

"I'm in," was all Peters said. "Order me a beer when she comes. I'm going to the restroom to puke."

Bolker sat there, contemplating his next move while Peters was gone. The Browning family deserved the best. Maybe that was the FBI, but he didn't think so. He had to find out more information on that drone that came in and obliterated the Browning house.

When Peters came back they sat there nursing their beers, neither of them hungry after the morning developments. They were talking back and forth, trying to figure the best recourse to find info on the mysterious drone and its origin.

They finally mustered the courage to go back to the office and relinquish the files the FBI demanded. It was always tough; the people in these files were real people. In the course of investigating, they'd come to know the victims' lives, their strengths and weaknesses, and the families left behind. It was personal with them, that's why they did this kind of work. This was going to be like divorcing or abandoning family. They walked into the office with heavy hearts.

CHAPTER 10

The Memorial Service

He had been working on the computer all afternoon. It was time to shut it down and get something to eat. Abby's Place wasn't open, so he walked out of the front of the hotel and headed in the opposite direction toward the clothing store where he bought clothes before. He couldn't wait for Monday, so he'd actually have his own place and could do some laundry.

There was a hamburger joint past the clothing store, and he went in for a bite. It wasn't Abby's cooking, but it was filling. He watched the people going back and forth in front of the store. He could feel the atmosphere. People stopped on the street to talk and laugh. It reminded him so much of home and his father. He liked it here, especially if Abby was part of here.

He walked out into the late afternoon to be part of the ambiance. People he didn't know smiled and greeted him as they passed, and he nodded back. He couldn't help but smile back. He drank in the essence of community as he made his way back to the clothing store. Maybe the guy who waited on him before could help him to know what clothes were appropriate for church around here.

He was greeted by a familiar face as he entered. Elias smiled and said, "Hi, how are you?"

The guy smiled back. "What can I do for you on this great Saturday afternoon?"

"I need to know what people usually wear to church around here."

"Which one?"

"The Christian church down a few blocks and south."

"You plan on going to the memorial for Alonzo tomorrow?"

"Yes, you know the place?"

"I'll be there too. We're casual by nature. Whatever you have is good enough."

"Well, all I have needs washed, and I'm living in a hotel right now," he said with a sheepish grin.

"You know, there's laundry service in the hotel."

"Yeah, I know," he lied; he'd never had to deal with this before. "I've just been busy."

"I've got just the thing for you if you are interested; follow me."

They went to the back of the store, and Elias picked out the colors and style the clerk steered him toward. Again, the clerk pulled his size out and pointed to the dressing room.

"Do I even have to try then on? You were right on last time."

The clerk grinned and said, "Suit yourself, what about shoes and underwear and socks?" as he walked toward the front of the store.

The guy was good. By the time Elias left the store, he had two large shopping bags full of clothes and shoes. The guy smiled as Elias left. He even opened the door for him.

"You come back now."

Elias strolled back to his hotel, just enjoying the walk. It never occurred to him that he didn't need the trees in his woods or the woodland creatures to be part of something bigger than him. He felt at home. He climbed the steps of his hotel with his packages. He was looking forward to going to church tomorrow with Abby and also looking forward to meeting her boys.

The Sunday sun was coming through the cracks in the curtains when he finally woke. He had to get ready. He showered and put on his new clothes. He combed his red hair and put on his new shoes. He was way early, so he went to the lobby to get some coffee and breakfast.

Time seemed to stand still on the old-fashioned wall clock in the dining area. He watched the people outside walking to church on the sidewalk. An occasional bus rolled by and stopped to pick up passengers. He wondered if Abby was ready yet.

Abby woke the boys and put them in the bath while she tidied up. She never got farther away than the next room, so she could make sure they weren't making a total mess or drowning each other. As they dried off and dressed, she hovered like a mother hen making sure their clothes were not inside out or on backward. She supervised the hair combing and shoe tying, the mother things that turn total chaos to order.

She fed them breakfast and let them play while she showered. She hadn't been so excited to attend church in a long while. She hoped Elias would show up today. She put on a special dress she hadn't worn for a year. It was one she had seen in the window of the dress shop that brought out the color of her hair and fit so well. She put on makeup for the first time in as long as she could remember.

Elias finished his coffee and got up to leave. He was still early, so he walked slowly. At five until nine he stood at the familiar door to the diner. He knocked on the door and waited for what seemed like an eternity. What if she had already gone? What if she had changed her mind? All kinds of insecure thoughts crept into his mind. Finally, he caught a glimpse of her approaching the door. She fumbled with the lock momentarily, and then the door swung open wide. He stood there speechless at this beautiful woman who stood before him. Her smile once again lit up his life!

"Come in."

He tried, but he was weak in the knees and afraid to move. When he recovered sufficiently to move, he stepped in and let the door close. He caught a whiff of her familiar perfume and his knees almost went away again.

"Wow, you look beautiful!"

Her heart skipped a beat. She hadn't heard those words for so long!

"Thank you!" she managed. "You look handsome."

He didn't agree with her but blushed at the compliment. "Thank you."

"I'll call the kids. Boys, come down here; there is someone I'd like you to meet."

They came clamoring down the stairs. She grabbed each one by the hand and led them over to Elias.

"This is the oldest one, Duane; he's six. This one is James; he's four. Boys, this is Elias."

The oldest boy eyed Elias with a "what are you doing here, we don't need you" kind of stare and an almost imperceptible nod. He pushed open the door and headed to the sidewalk.

"Don't get out of my sight!" his mom admonished, a little embarrassed by his response to meeting Elias.

Elias opened the door for her and James. He was hiding behind his mother, clinging to her dress. Elias caught him sneaking looks when he thought no one knew. They walked at a leisurely pace toward the church, talking and enjoying the cool, clear morning. Duane trotted ahead like a puppy. He grabbed the lamppost with one hand and went around and around it, then checked out the dead bug on the sidewalk, and then played don't step on the sidewalk crack. Always, he had Elias in the corner of his eye, checking him out, just one notch down from getting dressed down by his mother. He knew the limits and pushed them to the brink. When he did get yelled at, he stopped and looked Elias right in the eyes as he was being disciplined.

About halfway through their journey, James pushed his way between the adults as they walked. He didn't say anything, but he didn't take his eyes off Elias. Elias knew he was being scrutinized, but that didn't matter. In the back of his mind, he contemplated what his reaction would be to the service today. He hoped his desire to be here with Abby didn't end in disaster. He hoped he could handle the memorial to his father.

Duane reached the steps first. He bounded up them like he was racing an imaginary friend to the top. When he got to the top, he turned around and jumped up and down in triumph with his fists clenched and his arms up in the air.

The old, majestic church gleamed in the sun. The stained-glass front window bent the sun's rays into a rainbow of colors signifying a welcome to all, no matter what their circumstances. Abby reached the steps and grabbed the handrail with her right hand and James with her left hand and started up.

James would require a little patience, as he wasn't quite up to bounding up the steps like his big brother. It seemed like the natural thing to do as Elias put the little guy's hand in his and matched Abby step for step to the top of the stairs. When his challenge was over, James looked up at Elias and smiled in triumph. Elias noticed James's mother in his smile.

James tore free of his protectors and ran over to his brother, mimicking his gestures at the top of the stairs. Abby gave them that mom look and motioned them to come over and go in the door together with her and Elias. They ran over and screeched to a halt just as they were at the door. Elias thought back to his own childhood. He never walked anywhere. He was always at a dead run. It must be a boy thing. He smiled.

It took a moment to adjust to the light. A greeter handed them both a bulletin with a big smile and a handshake. The church was large. The tall ceilings all seemed to lead to the front of the church where a large illuminated cross hung. The cross seemed to emanate, "Welcome!" Abby led them to her usual pew. She slid across the pew far enough for Elias to be comfortable. Because this was a special service, the boys wouldn't have a separate children's church. Everyone seemed to know Abby. She got up and shook hands and hugged each one. Of course, they turned to Elias and extended their hands in greeting.

"And who is this?" they all asked.

"This is Elias Tobias Montague," she introduced over and over.

The guys shook hands in greeting and went back to being guys caught up in their own world. Elias wasn't offended, he understood the guy code. The women talked right up to the time the service was ready to start. He overheard two of them talking about how they thought it was about time Abby started going out again. After all, it had been a long time since the accident.

He grinned inwardly. James nestled himself between Abby and Elias. When he was situated, he looked up at Elias and grinned sheepishly. Elias smiled back. Abby gave him an apologetic grin. His look reassured.

The pastor rose and started the service.

"Welcome, one and all. Today we are going to do something different. Some of you will probably clap for joy, but I'm not going to preach today! Instead we are going to have a holograph of Alonzo Browning giving his most famous speech, the one that helped to start New Detroit and all the other pilot programs like it all over the country. With his Bible-based philosophy, he transformed a society without hope into one of hope. He transformed a society of poverty and despair to one of prosperity and self-sufficiency."

His tone changed to somber. "As you know, Alonzo Browning and his family perished in a house explosion a little over a week ago. Since the event, all our flags have been flying at half-staff, a fitting tribute to an unselfish, dedicated man. The news on the cause of the tragedy is very sketchy and vague now, but we have been praying for his family, especially David. There is a possibility that he survived the tragedy. Let us pray."

Elias didn't hear much of the prayer. He was fighting the sadness and grief that threatened once again to overwhelm him. The three-dimensional hologram started, but Elias still had his head down. He heard his father's booming voice and thought back to the times he'd accompanied his father all over the country with the rest of the family when they could go. He knew the speech by heart, but he was now hearing it for the first time as everyone else heard.

He slowly raised his eyes to the image. There was his father, preaching like he was still flesh and blood. Elias wanted to go up and touch him, tell him he loved him, tell him he was sorry. The grief spilled down his cheeks. Abby noticed and handed him a tissue from her purse. She studied his face as he discreetly tried to dry his tears. She put her hand on his shoulder. He felt the compassion and strength. He knew he would be all right as long as she was in his life.

Abby studied his face as she pondered her feelings. Not many men his age would show emotion and allow themselves to cry. Maybe his boyish attitude attracted her. He didn't seem to have a macho bone in his body. He seemed to accept her as she was, on an even basis without trying to dominate her. She said a small prayer for him and her and them.

He watched the hologram, studying everything and listening intently. He was searing his father's image in his brain. He would never have to say to anyone that he couldn't remember what his father looked like. For the first time in a long time, he said a prayer of thanks for this opportunity. The presentation ended, and the preacher took over. There was silence in the sanctuary until he spoke. He prayed to dismiss, and everyone rose slowly to leave. Elias was again lost in thought, remembering. The moment melted slowly for him. As the church emptied, he sat still lost in thought.

Abby was busy with the boys and her friends, undoubtedly explaining the newcomer in their midst. She gave him his time, as she studied his face. There was more to this man than he was telling her. She knew, she just knew. She didn't sense danger, but she felt the deep hurt he felt. He would tell her in his own time.

They got up and shuffled out of the pews into the pleasant afternoon. In the short time he had been there, he could feel the change in the weather. He looked at Abby to see what was in store next.

"We're having a church lunch and a get together in a few minutes, and my friends would love for us to stay, if you can stand the scrutiny," she grinned sheepishly.

He grinned back, letting her know he understood. "Sure."

They walked back to the kitchen area. The boys made a beeline to the playroom, over and under and around everything, burning off the energy that children waste with impunity. They went through a door where all the other children their age congregated in a room loaded with age-appropriate toys.

"Can you peek in on the boys once in a while? I'm going to help the ladies finish the lunch. It will take about a half hour. You can get acquainted with the rest of the people while you wait."

"Yeah, sure," he replied.

He walked over to the room with the kids and peeked inside when she turned to go to the kitchen. They were playing, oblivious to the outside world. He turned and approached a group of men talking at the edge of a table. One of them was the pastor. He rose and extended his hand.

"I'm Richard Wesley," he said as they shook hands.

"Elias Tobias Montague," he offered.

"Elias, we were discussing Alonzo Browning and what an impact he has made on our world by applying the principles that God put forth in the Bible. Come join us."

Elias sat down after the introductions were complete. He was still in awe of the opinion that people his father had touched had of him. This went far beyond the glowing epitaph that sends many a scoundrel to his reward. This was genuine, heartfelt, family. He listened intently as they debated the changes that Alonzo Browning had made and what direction they would go now that he was gone.

The conversation naturally turned to the subject of how he and his family died. One opinion was a natural gas explosion set off the chain of events causing the tragedy. Others held to a conspiracy theory that someone had planted a bomb to go off when they would be home. One thought it was a tremendous lighting strike.

Richard turned to Elias and asked, "You've been very quiet; what do you think?"

Elias wanted to scream at them, "THE REASON MY WHOLE FAMILY IS DEAD IS BECAUSE OF ME!" but he just said, "I don't know. I'm waiting for the true story to come out."

"Do you think we are actually going to know the truth?" one of the conspiracy pundits of the group blurted out.

Elias just shrugged his shoulders. He was saved from saying something he shouldn't when one of the ladies preparing the meal came out and announced that it was ready.

Richard got up and went to the front of the serving table and said grace before the meal. The shuffling of chairs dominated the din as families found one another and lined up to eat. He saw Abby come out and go to the playroom to retrieve her boys. He followed her to the room. She fussed over them for a second, straightening clothes and retrieving shoes.

Then she marched them off to the restroom to wash their hands for lunch. Elias followed them into the restroom and washed his hands. He smiled at their exuberance and remembered his own brother and how they used to interact when they were young. He smiled as they burst from the restroom. Abby shanghaied the boys and grabbed their hands and herded them to the food line.

They sat down at a table surrounded by people he didn't know. He knew by the end of the meal they would be friends, maybe even family. He thought about the impact he had had on the financial world and how he had changed technology. Nothing he had ever done could compare to the simple impact this small moment in time was having on him.

Abby placed a fork full of food into her mouth and started to chew. The look on her face said it all. When she caught him watching her, she put her free hand to her mouth like women do when they are embarrassed to be seen eating. He grinned and averted his eyes, so she wouldn't be embarrassed. He listened to the symphony of sound around him. He couldn't make out the conversations individually, but that didn't matter. They combined to produce the joy he had not experienced since his own family passed.

As the meal wound down and people started to leave, he gathered his plate and piled James and Duane's plates on his in an attempt to help Abby. She let the boys go back to the playroom while she and the people assigned to the cleanup tidied up the dining area. Elias felt compelled to chip in.

He cleaned tables and helped the men fold and put them on the racks for storage. He saw Abby take off her apron and exit the kitchen. They were putting the last tables away when she came out of the playroom with Duane and James in tow. She motioned for him to follow as she exited the church through the side entrance. Once outside, she herded the boys toward home.

"What did you think? That hologram was so lifelike, wasn't it?"

"That meal was great and yes, that hologram was very lifelike." His voice trailed off a bit with the last answer.

They walked along in silence, just enjoying being together.

Duane ran up to his mother and asked, "Momma, can we go to the park?"

"You know you have to go home and change clothes first."

"Ok."

He ran ahead so far that she had to yell at him to stop. Then he ran back. Then James ran ahead with him, doing his best to keep up with his big brother.

"Stop!"

The boys slowed to a walk and started bickering. As she and Elias caught up with them, she gave Elias an apologetic look. He saw so much of himself and his brother in these two boys, but he didn't have a category in which to put his emotions. As soon as they reached the door and Abby unlocked it, they bounded in and ran upstairs to change.

"Would you like to go with us?"

"Sure, I'd like that."

"I'll be right down; I'm going to change too."

"I'll be here." He smiled.

A few minutes later, the boys came down the stairs just like they went up, with Duane in the lead. He stopped on the second step and jumped to the floor and stuck the landing. Then James tried the same stunt and landed off balance on the floor. He got up and glanced at Elias with that "I wanna be just like my big brother" look. Abby came down gracefully and more dignified.

They headed out the door with the boys in the lead. The boys ran to the crosswalk at the corner and waited. They knew if they tried to cross without Mom, they would all just turn around and go home. A child's eternity passed before Elias and Abby got there so they could cross.

Once safely across, the boys walked, skipped, and jumped ahead. The park came into view another block down. As soon as they crossed the last street before the park, the boys headed straight to the park on a dead run. Abby and Elias found a bench where Abby could keep an eye on the kids at play.

"I'll be moving tomorrow," Elias said matter-of-factly.

"Oh, where to?" Abby asked with a little bit of concern in her voice.

"I've been assigned an apartment in Gatewood."

"That's pretty far away from here."

"How far?"

"About thirty blocks. I doubt if you'll be able to come to the diner on a regular basis now," she said with a hint of concern.

He smiled a wry smile and answered back with a twinkle in his eye, "Yeah, it is, but I don't know of anywhere else that has the kind of peach pie I like, so I guess I'm stuck.

He paused, and then added, "I'm going to be working IT at Envirowheels."

She smiled that smile at him. She knew he was very smart and was the kind of man who could provide well. She was embarrassed at herself for even thinking about that, no longer than she had known him.

"I start work on Wednesday."

They talked about things important to young people, things about future, things about present, and things about past. They were two robins in spring, dancing around each other on the quest to meet on common threads of life, weaving a tapestry of commonality that, when complete, would bind them.

The afternoon faded into evening. The boys played almost nonstop. Abby finally called them over to gather to leave. They reluctantly headed over to her bench. She brushed off as much playground as she could and announced to Elias that they needed to get back.

As they walked on the sidewalk home, the energy the boys displayed all day seemed to leave like a battery-operated toy running out of charge. Duane started to walk beside his mother step for step. He knew that it was futile at his age and size for him to ask to be carried, even though he secretly wanted to; he was exhausted. James had no such pride; he circled his mom with his arms outstretched, palms up in the universal "carry me" pose every child uses. Mom knew he couldn't make it home on his own legs.

Kids his age went flat out, not thinking of saving any energy for the trek home.

Mom obliged him. Elias saw the interaction and volunteered to carry James. Abby was tired, and she knew she wouldn't be able to carry him the whole way and handed James to Elias. James wasn't sure about Elias carrying him and didn't immediately settle down with his head on Elias's shoulder but realized that his chances were better of getting a free ride all the way home with him. He grinned at Elias and let his fatigue overcome his doubt as his head nestled onto Elias's shoulder. Abby slipped her hand through Elias's arm and looked up at him. Her cheek touched his bicep.

"Thank you."

He smiled as he looked into her eyes. His own fatigue vanished as he drank in the moment. Samson himself would not have the strength that Elias felt at that moment. James was asleep before the first street crossing. They walked in silence most of the way home. Words cannot convey what life sometimes portrays. They stopped in silence as Abby opened the door. Duane waited impatiently for the chance to bolt in the door and up to his room. Elias passed James over to his mother She put him down and gave him a pat on the behind.

"Go upstairs with your brother."

The little guy stumbled away up the stairs, still half asleep. Abby turned to Elias.

"Thanks for coming with us today. I don't know when the kids have had so much fun, and it was really nice of you to help so much with them."

She moved in close to him, and he knew it was his cue to kiss her. Even the computer geek that he was knew. There was that word again.

That's when their lips touched, and his mind went blank. He felt her arms around his neck as she reached up on tiptoes to kiss him. His bliss ended when she pulled away. He opened his eyes to see hers looking at him with rapture. In a moment, she came back to her Abby mom persona.

"I've got to get the kids ready for bed," she said as she slowly pulled back, her hands purposely brushing his chest.

He slowly backed out of the door, not wanting to lose her image. When he was outside, she locked the door and put her palm to the glass. He did the same as he backed away and turned to go. Her right hand rested on her heart as she climbed the stairs contemplating what had just happened.

He touched the wet spot on his shoulder where James had slobbered and seared into his psyche the feelings that were so foreign to him.

CHAPTER 11

His New Digs

He woke early and sat down at his computer. Sunday was fresh in his mind as he checked out the progress of his sleuthing. He had a data-gathering program he had created to track the progress of the Rothfellas' empire. They couldn't make change for a bitcoin without him knowing about it.

He needed to check out his new apartment. He exited the cloud and shut down his system. He was getting more and more information on the workings of the Rothfellas. He was learning about their weaknesses, their strengths, and the best way to do the most damage to them. Know your enemy! He felt empowered and at the same time uneasy. He was ashamed to admit to himself that he was just as vindictive as his enemy.

He decided to take a cab to his complex. He was unclear exactly where it was, and he still hadn't bought a phone. He called the lobby on the phone in his room and had the receptionist call a cab. This was going to be a first for him; he'd never ridden in a car with a human driver. He walked down to the lobby and waited. A red car marked "Cab" on its side pulled up. He loaded his computer gear and his belongings into the trunk and opened the back door and got in.

"Where to?" the driver asked.

"Gatewood apartments," he replied.

The cabbie flipped up a metering device and started off.

"How come you still have drivers in the cars?" he asked bluntly.

The cabbie smiled. He'd been asked the same question many times. "I make my living this way. I can provide the same service at a lower price as the driverless cars, because I don't have the overhead and the expense of the new state-of-the-art driverless cars. I also don't have to pay the monthly fees that the driverless owners pay for the network. The government has raised the fees so much in the past years that only big companies with a lot of volume can afford them. Besides, I own this cab. I take pride in what I do. Alonzo Browning believed that humans need to interact with one another. Machines have no passion or compassion. Instead of the machines becoming like us, we were becoming like them. You won't find a robot or an android taking a human's job in Brownstown. We're in this together."

"Oh," was all Elias could muster as he pondered what the driver had said.

He had heard his father say those same words in some of his speeches. He really understood it for the first time. He understood his father more every day he stayed in Brownstown.

"Here we are. You're on the left."

Elias looked the place over. It was old architecture, but the buildings looked new.

"Can you take me to Envirowheels?" he asked the driver.

"Sure, it's your coin." He grinned in the rearview mirror.

"A few blocks down the road, they came to a large warehouse with a parking lot full of cars in various states of disrepair.

"What's the deal on this company?" he asked the driver.

"Good company but it is having lots of computer issues. The company sold me this car. It was repossessed in Detroit, and Envirowheels acquired it with a lot of other abandoned vehicles at a sheriff's sale. The company y retrofitted the steering wheel and the pedals for me last year."

"I'm going to start work here on Wednesday."

"Great, where to now?" he liked fares like this, less down time and more meter time.

"Back to Gatewood, I need to check in with the office and get settled."

"Ok. Welcome to New Detroit. Hope your new start here went as well as mine did."

Elias removed his meager luggage from the trunk and paid the cabbie. He walked into the office and handed the receptionist his paperwork and paid his rent and deposit. The woman handed him the keys to the first apartment he had on his own, twenty-nine, Gatewood apartments. He walked down the sidewalk and found his new permanent residence.

When he opened the door, the smell of fresh paint welcomed him. The kitchen was small, but he didn't know how to cook anyway. The furniture was nearly new. The bedroom had a queen-size bed and a dresser but no linens. He forgot! He couldn't settle in until he got pots and pans and silverware and pillowcases and pillows and bed linens. The computer genius was getting overwhelmed. He'd never had to do this.

He wondered if Abby would help him. He needed a phone! He couldn't put it off any longer. Now he had one number he needed desperately to call, and that was Abby.

He went to the nearest bus stop and waited. When the bus came that would take him back to his old temporary neighborhood he got off and walked to the computer store. The guy was with a customer, so he browsed the newest phones.

The service rep walked over to Elias with the patent Brownstown smile and greeted him. "What can I do for you today?"

Elias had already picked out his phone, so he pointed it out to tech and said, "I need your minimum contract time and your maximum data plan."

The guy just nodded and started setting up the account. All he needed was Elias's bit-card and a signature of acceptance. He tried to make small talk, but Elias was in another world.

"Swipe your bit-card . . . And here's your new phone! Do you need any help with setup? If you have your old phone, I can transfer your data in an instant."

"My old phone was destroyed in a creek."

"Oh, well, I can't help you with that."

He handed the phone to Elias and said, "Thanks for the business!"

Elias walked out of the store and waved and smiled back at the clerk. He walked to Abby's Place. It was three and she would just now be closing for the day. As he walked down the street to the diner, he caught sight of Coy and Birdie walking into the diner. He entered just as they were being seated. Abby had already gone to the kitchen to get their pie and coffee. She smiled as she caught sight of him.

"You're early," she said to him as she served the couple.

He didn't reply until she walked over to his table. He was embarrassed that he didn't know how to set up his own apartment. He was considered a genius but that didn't always apply to the common-sense smarts that everyday living required.

"Abby, I need your help."

He said it with such an air of drama that she started thinking about the many scenarios that go through a woman's mind at this stage of a relationship.

"Sure, I'll help if I can," she replied.

What if he was going to ask for money or a place to stay, or bail money to stay out of jail? She had all her money tied up in the restaurant, and she wouldn't jeopardize her kids, no matter how she felt about him by letting him move in, and bail money was out of the question.

"I got my new apartment today, and I just don't know where to start. I don't have anything, like pots and pans or sheets and towels. I don't even have dishes or silverware. Would you go shopping with me, so I know what to buy? I'd take you to dinner wherever you want. I'm desperate!"

She was a little embarrassed by her thoughts about this sweet but naïve man. He obviously came from privilege if he was this helpless. Probably had androids to do everything for him, or maybe he had never lived away from home.

"I'd like nothing else than to go shopping with you, but I can't leave my boys. They'll be coming through the door any time."

Coy and Birdie were eavesdropping on the young couple's conversation. They talked among themselves for a minute and then Birdie spoke. "Why don't you let Coy and me watch the boys while you young people go out? We don't get to see our grandkids much since our son got transferred, and we would really enjoy it. You are always letting us come in after hours and enjoy our evenings, so let us help you."

"I think they would enjoy that! They don't get to see their grandmother much either. I'll go up and change and get them some toys and clothes ready. Send them up when they get here."

Abby hadn't been power shopping for a long time. Money was tight, and she was so busy with her business that she rarely got to go out at all. What a blessed change of plans. She hurried upstairs.

The boys bounded in the door and went over to Coy and Birdie. They always got hugs and questions about their day at school before they went upstairs every day.

The boys liked the old couple who hung around the diner in the afternoon. This day, Birdie motioned them over in that universal conspirator grandma manner and whispered in their ears about the possibility of coming to her house for a little while this evening while their mother went shopping. The boys' eyes lit up at the possibility of going on an adventure with Coy and Birdie, especially on a Monday night.

Abby descended the stairs carrying two bags for the boys. In those bags was everything that two boys would need to be away from their mother for the evening, and possibly for a week. Moms do that when they are not used to having their kids stay with someone else.

She was giving Coy and Birdie instructions on what the boys needed and what they could and couldn't do. She was still talking when they walked out of sight down the sidewalk. Birdie waved and reassured Abby that she had this under control.

Abby's attention turned to Elias. "Why don't you call a cab? I'll go and freshen up while we are waiting."

He got out his phone, went to the directory, and found the Red Cab number among the many cabs listed. He called, hoping to get the same guy as before. He liked the personal service he got with the real driver. Uber had gone driverless many years ago and wasn't any cheaper than this cab driver. He waited in anticipation for Abby to come down. He pondered how things just seemed to work out for the best here. He was glad she could help and was looking forward to dinner. He wasn't disappointed as she came into view.

"You look nice."

She smiled at the thought of spending the afternoon with Elias and not having to cook for a change, and, of course, shopping.

The cab pulled up and they got in. "Where to?" the cabbie asked as he turned the meter on.

"Dylands Department Store," Abby replied.

"There's something I have been meaning to ask you for a long time. Why doesn't Brownstown have big multinational department stores or grocery chains?"

"Alonzo set up our charter so that any corporation had to be based in Brownstown to do business here. The money generated here has to stay in the community. The big box stores were unwilling to do that. It opened a lot of opportunities for local businesspeople to compete. We might pay a little more, but we get the benefits of corporate involvement in our community."

"Oh," Elias said as he contemplated his father's wisdom.

"We need to make a list. Let's start with the kitchen," said Abby as she pulled out her phone and started typing. When she finished, she started on a list for the bedroom. By the time they reached the department store, she was ready. Elias paid the driver and walked behind her into the store. She was on a mission and he was dead weight.

He marveled at her efficiency and knowledge. He was just there to pay the bill and that was all right by him. She asked him to get a cart, as she also got one. This was going to take more than one cart. He followed behind her, answering questions like what size, what color, and what brand until his head hurt.

In no time, the carts were overflowing, and they were heading to the checkout. He called the cab, so it would be available when they rolled their treasures out the door.

"We just got the bare necessities today to get you set up. When you get settled, we can get décor items and picture frames and stuff that make a house a home."

He liked the sound of "we."

They waited outside for the cab. When it arrived, they loaded everything in the trunk and headed to his apartment. They carried the household goods into the apartment with the help of the cabbie. Elias gave him a nice tip when he paid the fare.

"Let's see a self-drive give that kind of service!" he thought as the cab pulled out.

Abby was already putting things away and the dishes and silverware in the dishwasher. as he walked in. He started opening packages and taking things to the appropriate room. She showed him how to properly put fitted sheets on the bed and how to make the pillowcases slide onto the pillows and then showed him how to wash them in his washer.. His home took shape in front of his eyes.

Even though he hadn't known Abby long, the thought crossed his mind that she would complete him; she would fill the gaps where he was lacking. He was lost in that thought when she brought him back to reality.

"So, where are you taking me to dinner?" she asked with that big smile. "You know I'm going to pick the most expensive place in town!"

"Any place you want, Abby! I'm so grateful that you came in here and did in two hours what I couldn't do in a week." He hugged her like he would never let go, picking her up off the floor and dancing out the door.

He called for the cab. When it arrived, they got in.

"Where to?" the cab driver asked.

"Anywhere the lady wants to go!" exclaimed Elias. He was giddy with her presence.

"Robinsons," was all she said.

"Yes, ma'am!" said the driver with a smile.

"What is this Robinsons?" asked Elias.

"It's just the best restaurant in New Detroit!"

"Do we need reservations?"

"I already made reservations before we left my place."

"Oh, ok, let's go."

As far as he was concerned, any restaurant was fine as long as Abby was there. This was something special. It was the first time they had been alone together on anything resembling a real date. The food didn't matter to him; it was the atmosphere. This was a chance to have Abby's undivided attention and to learn everything he could about her. Someday he hoped to be able to go to Robinsons for a special anniversary and sit at their special table and hold hands and play "remember when." He had never felt this way about anyone! Of course, he hadn't known her long enough to even think that way, but he couldn't help himself.

Abby was surprised when he helped her with her chair at the table. He truly was a gentleman. She couldn't help herself; she had been thinking about the future. It was something she couldn't easily fathom after her husband was killed. Was it possible she could have that happiness again? He put his hand over hers and asked about her family. She couldn't help feeling déjà vu, her husband had done the same thing on their first date.

They talked about everything and nothing. She thought about Coy and Birdie, not because of the boys but because of the dynamics in their relationship. She saw the tenderness and love, the laughter and joy, the way they completed each other. She wanted that but thought all was lost on that fateful night when she was widowed. Did she dare dream of happiness again?

CHAPTER 12

The Corporate World

Elias spent Tuesday setting up his computer office in his new place. He called for utilities and network activation for his computers. His new state-of-the-art computer desk would be delivered Saturday. He would have to visit his favorite computer store and order some special computer chips and get another monitor.

It occurred to him that he should check in at his new job and get acquainted with the place he would be spending his days from nine to five, five days a week. This was something new to him. He had always set his own hours and been in charge of his own destiny.

When he walked out the door, he took note of the time, so he would know how long it took him to walk to work. He would take a bus on the way back and see if the bus schedule was compatible to his schedule, in case of bad weather.

Twenty-nine minutes later, he was at the entrance to Envirowheels. He gave the guard at the gate his name and the code that Daniel had provided in his packet and explained why he was there. The guard called the Human Resource department and a few minutes later, someone was sent to the gate to escort Elias in.

"Hello, Mr. Montague; welcome to Envirowheels. We didn't expect you until tomorrow. My name is Tabatha. I'll show you to the IT department and introduce you to Darious Miller, who will be in charge of bringing you onboard his team."

Elias shook her hand and introduced himself, even though she already knew who he was. "I wanted to get a head start on my orientation, so I could start informed and ready tomorrow."

"A word to the wise, Mr. Montague; we already had that learning curve built in to your orientation tomorrow. I sense that you have never been in this kind of corporate environment before, so I'm going to tell you up front that we all have to be team players. This is a very structured workplace, and we have to follow the rules."

Elias didn't know if he would like it here. "I appreciate the information. You're right. I've never been in this environment. I've always been a freelance contractor, but that is getting more difficult with every government regulation."

"I think you'll like Darious, he's good at putting people at ease. It seems to be more difficult to get knowledgeable people in computer science positions. He's had a hard time lately with glitches in the self-drive sensor systems we supply to the auto industry."

She smiled and put him at ease. They entered a large, well-lit structure cordoned off into small group settings with computer monitors as far as the eye could see. He felt at home immediately. Darious's office was in one corner with his desk facing out at a forty-five degree angle, so he could see the entire floor. There was no door on his office. Over the entrance was written, "Yesterday is gone, and tomorrow is not promised, so make today great!"

"Darious, this is Elias Tobias Montague. He is your new team member starting tomorrow. He's the MIT grad we were expecting. Elias, this is Darious Miller, tour team leader."

Darious was a middle-aged man with a large frame, which was still as intimidating as it was in his college years when he played offensive guard on the four-time national champion Spartans football team. He had a quick smile and a get-the-job-done attitude. Elias liked him immediately.

"If you two will excuse me, I have work to do," she said as she left them.

They shook hands and exchanged pleasantries.

"MIT, eh? I'm Michigan State. Go Spartans!" he grinned at Elias and asked, "Would you like to tour the building?"

"Sure."

They walked around to a section that Darious described as research and development.

"You'll be working here," he said, pointing at a work station on his right. "We won't get into the details today, but we have a glitch in our sensor system that seems to defy definition, let alone correction. It's got me pulling my hair out. Maybe Mister MIT can show us the error of our ways." He grinned at Elias as he slapped him on the back.

"Eight sharp, tomorrow morning. We have a meeting at nine to introduce you to your team and help you get a feel for how things are done and what needs to be done. I have a meeting in twenty minutes, so I'll show you HR, where you can go ahead and get your security badge to get in and be ready to hit it tomorrow early."

Elias went through the process and obtained his official photo ID that allowed him access to the building. When he finished, he exited into the sunlit day, not a cloud in the sky. He hoped his time here would be as bright. He walked to the bus stop and timed his ride home. He looked up the bus schedule on his phone to see when it left from his stop in the morning. He was ready for tomorrow.

He didn't get off at his apartment stop. Instead he went to Abby's Place. He had a lot to share with her.

—∞—

Wednesday morning, he woke to his phone alarm at six. He wanted to be sure and board the bus in time. He dressed for work with a little butterfly dancing in his belly. He ate a bowl of cereal as he watched the news on his computer. He wanted to see if there was any news on the investigation into his family's tragedy. He thought for sure something would break after he sent the video from his cameras. The only thing was a one-sentence report about the FBI getting involved.

He hadn't checked his data for days. With the things going on in his life, it didn't seem as all-consuming as it once did. He felt a little remorse. He'd check tonight. It was seven-fifteen, and he would have to catch the next bus, so he put everything away and locked the door as he strolled down the street. As he walked, he noticed the days were getting shorter.

After the uneventful bus ride, he walked through the employee entrance at ten minutes until eight and made his way to his area and sat down at his desk. As the other employees strolled in, one by one they said hi or nodded his way. One woman even came over and introduced herself. He nodded back and returned their smiles and greetings. Everyone settled into their areas. Then Darious came in the door.

"Good morning, everyone; meeting in one hour, come prepared. Elias, I need to see you in my office."

"You wanted to see me?"

"Yes, Elias, I need to give you the codes and passwords you will need to get into the system. I want you use the remaining time before the meeting to get a feel for what we're up against here. We need to go back to the beginning and check everything to see what we are missing."

"Ok. I'll scan over the data as much as I can."

He sat down at his computer and logged onto the project. He spent the next half hour getting familiar with the code, then headed to the meeting. As the workers filed into the meeting room, he wondered how they would receive him. He was used to being the odd man out, a loner. People had agendas; he didn't. He lived for the challenge and the solution, everything to him was black and white. He realized he sometimes stepped on toes, because he didn't understand office politics. He would try to be quiet and listen and learn.

Darious called the meeting to order. "Everyone, this is Elias, the newest member of the team. Starting over here on my right, please introduce yourself."

As they went around the table, he rose and shook hands. His memory meme kicked in as he remembered every name instantly. He associated the first thing he noticed about each person and added the name to the memory.

"Let's get down to the problem at hand," commanded Darious. "I'll do a lot of review for all of you for Elias's sake."

He introduced the problem again, as it seemed he had done for the past six months since the new program came out. Elias listened intently to his presentation. Around the room, he noticed what seemed like different levels of interaction, from apathy to total engagement. He was forming opinions as to who he could approach as an ally and who was just there because they needed the money. He had questions already and wanted to know who could answer them.

"In the handout today is the program dissected into segments again. I want you to go over your assigned segment to check it again. Everyone has been assigned a different segment than last time."

An audible groan emanated from the room. Elias looked over his assignment as he strolled back to his desk. This was going to be a challenge.

The rest of his day was spent testing different scenarios on the computer simulator. When he looked at the time, it was already seven o'clock. It happened every time he was involved in a project—he lost all track of time. Everyone was already gone. He left the building and decided to walk home. He was lost in thought when he arrived at his apartment.

He called Abby to let her know he wouldn't be at her place tonight. He made himself a sandwich and wolfed it down with a soft drink chaser. He plopped on his bed and stared at the ceiling, absentmindedly thinking about the software problems. He couldn't help it, he was obsessed. He dozed off, only to wake to his morning alarm.

Thursday, he formulated his solution to the Envirowheels software problems. He knew that the Friday morning meeting was going to give him a chance to introduce his findings to everyone. He spent the whole day researching data and preparing his findings, so he could present it to everyone in a way they could understand.

—⚅—

Darious came into the room Friday to preside over the meeting. He wasn't optimistic that anyone had been able to identify the glitch. They had been after this bug for months, and so far it had been elusive.

"Good morning, everyone, hope you all have wonderful plans for the weekend coming up. Right now though, we need to focus on the problems at hand. I'm going to ask the same question I've asked every Friday for as many months as I can remember. Has anyone identified any reason that our software should be acting like it does?"

Elias waited. Everyone was silent, distracted, hoping someone, anyone, would come forward and rescue them from this purgatory. Darious sat in frustration. It was crunch time. Corporate had given them all the time they could to get a viable product out the door. If the software couldn't be fixed in the next four weeks, the company was going to pull the plug on this whole department, and a lot of people were going back to the unemployment lines. Darious rubbed his forehead in silence.

"Mr. Miller, I think I have something, if you would allow me to present it."

"The name's Darious, MIT. Have at it. It's the fourth quarter, and we're losing by a field goal. We have time to throw one more Hail Mary pass to the end zone to win the game."

Elias started in by wheeling a large monitor to the end of the table where everyone could see, and then he started his presentation. "As far as I can tell, the software we have is flawless."

Everyone in the room perked up.

"Last year, the company decided to change suppliers of the sensors that provide the system with data. These new sensors have a different, deeper curvature to the lenses. This creates a void so deep that our current system can't pick it up. As you know, the sensors are like a fly's eye with many facets that have to work together. See this pencil? When it is directly in front of me, I can see the image clearly. But as I pull it over to the side, my peripheral vision distorts it until I can no longer make out anything but a yellow blur. This is the area our program in lacking.

We have to convert this blur into a pencil again, so the sensors can convert the signal received into a signal that the control servos can understand. The angle of these new lenses is not as precise as the last manufacturer's lenses. See on the screen where the curved line representing the curve of the lenses intersects? It forms an X with the two ends not meeting. We have to make sure that the data from the peripheral ends of the lenses come together and form a continuous V wave where the ends meet. Then they can be picked up by the software and converted to a straight line like a panoramic camera creates a picture out of many exposures."

He paused and asked, "Does anyone have any questions before I go on?"

When no one answered, he continued, "We need to create an algorithm to handle the discrepancy in the data. I can write the algorithm part if you all can work with me and join the software program together with my algorithm. It will save the company millions in saved inventory and we get to keep our jobs!"

His feeble attempt at humor was ignored, but he could feel the excitement build in the room. For the first time in a long time, they had a common, achievable goal.

Darious's mood lightened considerably. "You pull this off, and I'm buying at Robinsons!" he exclaimed.

"Make the reservations for a week from next Friday," Elias said with a little swagger in his voice.

—∞—

The team worked diligently to understand his concepts and get their code to run efficiently with his. He was in his element. He spent long days formulating his algorithm and trying to explain it to his coworkers. By Friday, they were ready to test the new software. That kind of turnaround was unheard of in this business. Elias was the driving force behind the speed of their success. They spent the next week debugging the system.

Thursday, they did another test run, and it was flawless. They changed the parameters on the sensors and the system adjusted. They changed back to the original sensors and the system was still flawless. This meant the software could be adapted to all kinds of applications. Darious invited his corporate leaders to watch the program software work. The leaders were so impressed that they not only bought the team dinner, but they also added a nice bonus for the whole team!

Friday, Darious called Elias into his office. "Well, MIT, you did it! You fixed the problem in a few weeks, and we had been working on it for months."

"We all did it. I couldn't have written that much code in that short of time without the whole team."

"You're right. I'm glad you have that attitude—a team player all the way. I've been working on a project for the company that would fit you perfectly. It is cutting-edge stuff that no one else has ever done."

"You've got my attention. What is this all about?"

"Do you remember an inventor named Nikola Tesla? He was the pioneer of electric power. He harnessed the power that is all around us. This power is free, so no company was interested in backing him. In fact, his first real attempt at harnessing his discovery for the good of humans, building a transmission station called Wardenclyffe Tower, was torn down. Powerful men who had invested in the power grid took him down."

"Yeah, I know the story well," replied Elias.

He knew the story all too well. His whole family had perished because of his attempt to change the established order. The hectic, all-consuming project that he had been a part of gave him some respite from his grief. He had managed to tuck it away and wall it up inside, but now the Tesla story broke down his flimsy wall and allowed the loneliness and grief out again. He needed to see Abby tonight. He'd call her after the lunch at Robinsons.

"What is this top-secret project?"

"We have managed to reproduce his experiments and produce unlimited energy from the different electric charges between space and earth. We witness this energy in the form of lightning every day. Ever thought of taming a bolt of lightning? That is essentially what we are trying to do. We have had some success but, again, our software is not sufficient to handle every situation. Our craft is subject to failure at the whim of the slightest particle charge difference in the atmosphere, especially around unsettled weather like thunderstorms. If we could work out the problems, we could possibly have unlimited transportation and free energy for all humankind."

"What do you mean by craft?"

"We have adapted the energy generator to power a personal craft that is the next generation of transportation. It can take off vertically from any location that doesn't have any overhead obstructions and travel on the waves of energy I was talking about."

"Why haven't I heard about this?"

"For the same reason that Tesla and the many who believed in his discoveries were silenced, it was and is greed. Not until Alonzo allowed us the freedom to explore this avenue, and provided the funding for this corporation through the Browning Foundation, has any research been formally carried out.

If the solar energy manufacturers, or the wind turbine manufacturers, or the lithium battery manufacturers, or the power companies, or the government got wind of this, we would be shut down or the lab would meet with an 'accident' and be destroyed. It has happened before, so what I'm telling you cannot go beyond this room, understood?"

"Yes, sir, I understand completely. When can I see this craft?"

"We have to get you the proper clearance from headquarters. That shouldn't be a problem after what you have already done for this company. I'll expedite the process after our lunch at Robinsons. We have come to the end of our funding, so we are trying to get more. I don't know how the foundation is going to react to this top-secret clandestine project after Alonzo's death."

Elias got up to leave. He reached out to shake Darious's hand.

"Thanks for everything," he said.

"Hey! It's me that should be thanking you."

Darious didn't realize what the input about Alonzo and the lengths that he and the Browning Foundation had gone to for the people meant to Elias. He was learning more and more about the greatness of his humble father. He was so glad he didn't check out and go to the beach or the mountains. This interaction with his father's dream was the best therapy he could have. His father was alive in him and all around him in spirit. He walked out of Darious's office.

The lunch at Robinsons was wonderful. The camaraderie and interaction he felt with these people was a new experience for him. He had always been detached from his workers in his own corporations, because he was always the top dog. It was a new experience to be a part of a team, to belong.

That evening at Abby's Place, he couldn't contain his excitement. He didn't remember ever being this happy and joyous, even before the tragedy. He wasn't really hungry, so he just asked for some peach pie and sweet tea. He wanted to share his excitement with the only person he felt really close to. Abby sat down across from him with her own pie and sweet tea. They savored the pie and each other.

Coy and Birdie looked on. They both agreed that the two young people across the room reminded them so much of their own young romance. They knew from the start that they would always be together through anything that life had to offer, even if it meant being physically apart for a time, such as when Coy had to serve in the Navy. They knew that their time together was growing short. In the turmoil that was the world today, it was comforting to the old couple that what they had would perpetuate in the form of this young love.

Almost in unison as Coy reached over to caress his love's hand, Elias did the same. Elias told Abby of his triumph, with the excitement of a schoolboy. She loved his enthusiasm and listened as he recounted his experience of the day. She let him ramble on, listening intently. She had missed this so much since her husband's death. She missed the sharing and the oneness that she once had. She glanced at the old couple who had shared so much with her just by being in her life. She hoped she was looking through a mirror of time at her own future.

CHAPTER 13

The Craft

Elias was sitting at his desk early Monday morning, waiting in anticipation of the next new adventure. He had been creating the "craft" in his mind all weekend. When Darious arrived and summoned him to his office, he had butterflies in his stomach.

"I've got your clearance right here," he said. "Let's go explore the future."

Elias followed him past the office complex down a long hallway that led to a door that looked like the front entrance to a bunker. He was instructed to place his eye so the machine could read his retina. Then he had to place his badge and his fingerprint on the pad. Five seconds later, the door clicked and opened slightly. They pushed their way through the door. When they were inside, a sensor shut the mammoth door behind them. There was a click and the sound of tumblers turning. They were entombed in the research lab.

Technicians greeted Darious as they passed. He introduced Elias to everyone. They walked through the lab to a large door that again required security. On the other side of the door in a ten-story room as large as a football field were three machines the size of a large pickup truck. They resembled large sunflower seeds still in the shell. There were no wings or engines or seams anywhere. Two were resting on their landing gear, which consisted of one retractable support in front and one on each side of the back. All three had pads instead of wheels.

The third machine seemed to be suspended in midair. A slight hum came from the suspended machine. When Elias approached it, he felt a sensation like the instant right after a lightning strike in a thunderstorm. The air seemed to have a different smell and feel to it. It was called ionization. He ran his hand down the fuselage, trying to feel a seam or a flaw.

"What is this material?" he asked.

"This is a proprietary composite substance that is lighter and stronger than steel," replied Darious. "It starts as a liquid and is extruded through a computer-controlled, three-dimensional printer. It is then cured for a week under ultraviolet light."

There were technicians milling around, checking the hull with different recording sensors. Elias walked around with them asking questions and observing. He came back to Darious.

"I don't feel any heat. How is that possible?"

"This reactor runs on what we just call Tesla energy. It has a lot of the same properties as Thomas Edison's direct current electricity, only it doesn't produce heat. We found in the process of making electricity that this was produced as a byproduct. When we run ground cables in the installation of any electric power installation, we are essentially moving this energy into the ground. We decided to harness this energy instead of neutralizing it."

"How does it work?"

"We imbed in the hull on top and bottom an aluminum alloy sheet that creates a charged capacitor. We vary the charge in relation to the charge in the air around it. That's why you feel the sensation of ionized air around it."

"How do you get it to move forward?"

"When Tesla built his Wardenclyffe Tower, he had in mind to transmit radio waves and unlimited energy. We are the equivalent of that tower, although we move on those waves instead of remaining stationary. We are limited only to the speed of the waves and the physical strength of the hull of these ships, in theory."

"Have you actually flown any of these?"

"Only in the lab, the problem we have is the limitations of our software. Because the charge in relation between the atmosphere and the earth is always in flux, we have been limited to flight inside this building. We can control the charge in here, so we can control the height of the machine, but outside we are at the mercy of the earth and the atmospheric charge in any given nanosecond."

"How do you get inside?"

"Let me show you."

Darious walked over to the first stationary machine and touched the hull with his palm in an area that was a slightly different color than the rest of the hull. A ramp lowered out of the bowels of the machine with a whir and a thump.

"Come on, let's get aboard."

Darious climbed the stairs and disappeared inside, followed closely by Elias. The interior resembled a large, self-drive car, except four seats were aligned along the walls like a small aircraft, two on each side with an aisle down the middle. There were two seats side by side facing a large, curved computer screen in the front. There was a keyboard in front of both chairs with a large, ball-shaped mechanism embedded on the armrest resembling a large, roll-on deodorant applicator.

Darious touched the top of the headrest on the left seat, and it swiveled around to face him. He got in and moved the seat back into flight position. Elias touched the other seat, and it did the same. When they were situated, Darious placed his hand on the ball. The control screen came to life. He tapped the screen and a slight hum started to emulate from the top of the craft. After about ten seconds, he touched a three-dimensional grid resembling a Rubik's Cube on the screen and entered "twenty meters."

The craft immediately rose twenty meters off the landing pad and hovered motionless. He rolled the ball that his hand was resting on forward, and the craft eased forward slowly. He rolled the ball to the right, and the machine banked right and traveled around the hangar to the right until it was back in its original position. He did the same thing to the left. When the machine was back in its original position, he entered zero and the machine settled gently to the ground in the exact position it started.

"Wow, where do I sign up?!"

"You are already signed up. We need your expertise and genius on the computer. Do you think you could write an algorithm for this like you did for the sensor problem?"

"Yes, this is a very similar problem. The craft could be buffered by a force shield that controls the ionic charge to allow the system in the craft to manipulate the Tesla charge. I'm just worried that it would take too much power to accomplish this."

"I'm sure you can work it out, MIT," Darious said with a grin. "I've got to get back to the IT lab and get started on our next project. The people on the floor are very dedicated to this project and will answer any questions you have. You will have to go through the flight training, after which they will give you the code and show you how to install your fingerprints on the machine so you can fly it. Report back to me on Friday afternoon."

Elias was awestruck. He had no idea what his father and the Browning Foundation were involved in. He couldn't help but swell with pride at what his wealth had and would create. Something had drawn him here. People he needed were put in his path at the right time. He couldn't explain why.

He knew the power of God, but he had a hard time justifying all the suffering in the world with a God that claimed to be loving. Yet he felt God in his life. Why had his family been taken? Why was he made to stay behind and suffer the loss? In the midst of all his technological savvy was tremendous suffering. Technology was supposed to be the panacea, the promise of a better life. Still his suffering continued. Why? He tried to put his feelings back in his vault and lock the door. Maybe this was the breakthrough that humankind, and he, needed to turn off the suffering.

He turned to the nearest technician and started asking the questions he needed answered so he could once again throw himself headlong into the project. Maybe this would be the tipping point, the pot of gold at the end of the humans' troubled and dark rainbow.

Weeks flew by. Three months into the project, and countless failures in the computer simulations and countless disappointments in the progress of the project, the unthinkable happened. The funding ran out for the fiscal year. The board of directors of Envirowheels was reeling from the decline in its stock price and the decline in earnings caused by the computer and sensor glitches that Elias and his team had fixed. The company was scrambling to meet its earnings predictions for the year. The stockholders were demanding action, so the logical corporate response was to trim unprofitable programs. The top-secret Tesla energy craft was the first to get the ax.

Elias was sitting in Darious's office, feeling dejected and depressed. He was talking to Darious about the progress in his weekly report when Darious broke the news. Elias thought they were just days away from success, but he had felt that way on many occasions, and the new methods never panned out. Still, he believed, there had to be a way to keep the project up and running.

Darious tried to be upbeat about the company's future by spouting the official company rhetoric. He stopped mid-sentence and sat down at his desk. "This is bull! I started that project right after Envirowheels was formed. Alonzo convinced the Browning Foundation to fund Envirowheels, and he was very excited about the Tesla craft. I think if he hadn't been killed that the company would get behind us again. But the new projects in Chicago and San Francisco have put the Browning Foundation under a lot of financial stress. New Detroit is the only city that has a balanced budget so far. The others are about three years behind us in their five-year plans. That means they are still a large financial strain on the foundation."

Elias sat in silence, lost in thought. "Has the company tried to find a buyer for the project?"

"Under the circumstances, it is throwing everything not essential for survival overboard to try to save the sinking ship. Given the red tape and the questions the new government would undoubtedly pose, I think the leaders are taking the easy way out. They want to quietly shut it down and liquidate any assets and absorb the losses.

"Just out of curiosity, what do you think they would take for the whole project, including proprietary license and all patent rights?"

"More than everyone combined makes in this company in years. Guys like us can't just buy something like this, MIT! It would take too long to raise the funding. They are giving us three months to shut down."

Elias didn't say anything for a long time. The two of them sat fuming in silence, not knowing what their next step would be. Elias was contemplating something that might put him in jeopardy again. He trusted Darious. The man had always been a straight shooter with him. One thing bothered him—Darious was a company man, loyal to the end. He weighed the risk of revealing his identity to give credence to a financial offer he was about to make. He thought better of it.

"Can we take a walk, Darious? There is something I need to discuss with you off the record."

"Sure, we're getting nothing done sitting here staring into space. I could use some fresh air about now."

They walked in silence for a long time. Elias was contemplating whether he should do this at all. His life was in a good place right now. Why would he jeopardize everything for a long shot like this? His father believed in this project, and so did he. Maybe that's why. He decided to feel out the company and see if it was interested in selling this part of the business before he went out on a limb and told Darious who he really was.

"I have some relations who are venture capitalists. They might be interested in backing this project. Would you find out if the board of directors would sell?"

Darious stopped abruptly. He studied Elias's face to see if he was serious. He wouldn't even consider that suggestion from anyone else Elias's age, but this kid was different. He seemed much older, wiser than his years.

"We're talking millions of bitcoin here, plus at least the same for operating capital. Are your relations up for that?"

"I'll ask them, if you will find out if it could be bought."

They walked on, each trying to stifle their excitement for something that was a long shot at best. They talked about potential and risk, and odds that the craft would ever fly outside a controlled atmosphere. Darious was the earth and Elias was the sky. They were yin and yang searching for opportunity and truth. Somewhere between the two were Envirowheels' craft and possibly the future of aviation.

That night, Elias did something he hadn't done since his father died; he checked his own finances. Most of the time, it didn't matter to him how much he was worth. One man can only spend so much, but this was different. He needed to know if he could actually afford to acquire and fund this research company until it could produce a viable, sellable product without affecting the Browning Foundation. His Dubai company seemed to be the best suited for what he had in mind. He had twenty-five-million bitcoin in reserves he could tap into. Now, if Darious could come through with the board of directors of Envirowheels, they would be in business.

The next week, Darious came strolling through the complex in the middle of Friday afternoon. Elias knew something was up, because Darious never visited unannounced. He had the butterflies again as Darious approached. Darious tried to look somber as he neared Elias, but he couldn't hide his excitement.

"The board of directors is willing to entertain any offer at the present time. I did some snooping through the books for this project and the company has five million in bitcoin in research money and another million in fixtures and equipment. Rent on this much industrial space would run ten-thousand bitcoin a month, if we wanted to stay."

"It looks like we need to get a good team of corporate lawyers as soon as possible!" Elias said, elated, anxious, and scared at the same time. He was really investing in his own confidence and ability as a problem solver as much as buying a company. "Darious, will you come on board as the CEO of Dubai International Research Company, if we get this deal finalized? You have a vested interest in seeing this project through, not to mention stock options and the possibility to become very wealthy. I know technology and computers, but I need the day-to-day operating decisions to be made by someone I can trust."

Darious looked at him for a minute. "What do you mean I?"

Elias was busted. He never was a good liar. He decided to come clean with Darious about who he was and his real reason for being in Brownstown. "Can we walk?"

"Yes, of course. I suppose next you are going to tell me you are an independently wealthy tycoon or something, eh, MIT?"

"Pretty much," Elias grinned. "Come on, old man, I have a fairy tale to spin along with your head."

As soon as they cleared the gate, Elias started his odyssey from the time he made his first million to creating the Browning Foundation to the tragedy that killed his family. Alonzo was a common thread that they both had before they knew each other. Darious was speechless.

"There is one other person who knows who I am. That is the truck driver who I made an accomplice of by stowing away in his truck. You must never tell anyone what I've just told you. Abby doesn't even know who I really am. I didn't want to put her and the boys in harm's way by just knowing me. Promise that you will tell no one!"

"Of course, I won't!" Darious said after he recovered from all the things he'd just heard. "So, are you going to be my supervisor?"

"Dubai International will be your employer, and I own the biggest share of the company, along with my siblings who are no longer with us. I am offering you part owner of a company that stands on the threshold of revolutionizing the whole world. How can we quibble over who is a supervisor? I get creative freedom, which is what I crave, and you get all the headaches of running a big corporation—sounds fair to me!"

Elias was grinning from ear to ear. Darious knew that this was a long shot, but he had almost as much confidence in Elias as Elias did. This rich, white kid from Indiana had something special. He couldn't put his finger on it; it was just that everyone he touched seemed to be elevated to a different level. Most people who had been through what he had gone through would be hiding in a corner, curled up in a fetal position in a mental ward, or so bitter they would be toxic to touch.

Yet, here he was offering a middle-aged black guy—who had to fight his way through the mean Detroit streets full of pushers and pimps and gangs just to get to school—a position most executives could only dream of. He thought of the sacrifice his mother had made for him and his brothers over the years. She would not let him fail. With her last minutes on this earth, she motioned him to her side. She grabbed a handful of his shirt and pulled his face close to hers.

"Darious, it's up to you! You've got to work harder. You've got to be better. You've got to rise above the racism and the pushers and the users and be ready. Good things will happen to you, I just know!"

She died a short time later. She never saw him receive his high school diploma or his scholarship to Michigan State. She never saw him play for the national championship, four years in a row, or walk across the stage at Michigan State with his degree, but she was always with him in everything he did. She was right. Darious didn't hesitate. "I accept your proposal, MIT!"

—⁂—

The months that followed were filled with lawyers and negotiations and everything it takes to form a multinational company. Darious poured everything he had into his position at Envirowheels. He didn't want even the hint of impropriety as he transitioned from one company to the other. He was still a team player, but he knew he was about to be traded.

Three months later, Darious and Elias were ready to launch the new separate venture. That's lightspeed in legal time. Because this was a distress sale and not a merger, both sides were able to come to a quick agreement. Darious had insisted on keeping separate and accurate expenses from day one, when Alonzo helped him launch the Tesla project for Envirowheels. Now he would bring that same integrity and expertise to Dubai International.

Elias had been working diligently on the control problems the craft faced but was making little headway. Still he was excited to finally ensure the future of this venture. Darious and Florinda, his wife, along with Elias and Abby went out to Robinsons to celebrate. Elias was positive that with its new CEO, Dubai International would be a world-changing company.

CHAPTER 14

The Revelation

By the end of January, Elias was at the end of his rope. He'd tried everything he could think of. He had tweaked the software and changed the sensors, and nothing seemed to work. Darious was getting worried, along with Elias. He was worried about Elias, who seemed sullen and testy. Elias spent way too many hours at work, and his obsession was taking its toll. The Friday meeting was not going well. One of the technicians suggested that Elias try a different approach and then proceeded to describe a procedure Elias had tried until he'd beat it to death.

"Don't you even listen?" Elias screamed. "We tried that three weeks ago and it didn't work!"

Elias's face was red and the veins in his neck were bulging. He was pacing up and down the room like a caged animal. Darious got up and put himself in Elias's path.

"Elias, that was unprofessional and uncalled for. This man was out of town during that meeting and was unaware of what went on. He should have been briefed but that didn't happen. I suggest you apologize."

Elias looked at the hulk of a man in front of him and calmed down. He knew Darious was right. He took a few deep breaths to calm himself and went over to the guy and extended his hand.

"Sorry, man. I was totally out of line. It won't happen again."

"No problem. I'll be sure and get a briefing if I ever miss another meeting."

Darious motioned them to all stand. "I'm going to offer a prayer for guidance and wisdom in this project, something we should have been doing from the start."

He bowed his head and began, "Dear Lord, please give us wisdom and patience as we go through the trials of this project and through everyday life. Let us know your will and be centered in it always. Amen." The men chorused, "Amen."

"Now, Elias, I don't want to see your face here until Monday morning! Go to Abby's and hang out, relax, and be ready to hit it next week. Leave, NOW!"

Elias walked out of the room, ashamed of his actions. Darious was right. He had put this project ahead of everything and that had to change. He checked out and walked out into the brisk, cold, January wind.

The bus was a welcome, warm place to reflect as he rode to Abby's. Doubt was creeping into his psyche. His confidence was waning. Maybe he was wrong. Always before, he could work through a problem while everyone else was trying to understand it. He hadn't been this low since his family died.

He got off at the familiar bus stop and trotted down to Abby's Place. It was three o'clock, and she would be closing. He came bursting through the door, dancing with the cold. He was glad that one customer was still lingering, and Abby hadn't locked the door yet.

It had been way too cold for Coy and Birdie to venture out, so he had called when he was close. He sat down at their booth and waited to see Abby's smiling face come through the kitchen door. The last patron got up to pay his tab and the waitress came over to check him out.

She waved and smiled at Elias as she walked through the kitchen.

"Hey, Abby, Elias is out here," she informed as she grabbed her coat to leave. "See you tomorrow morning."

Abby came out and sat down to catch her breath for a few minutes. "You're early."

"Yeah, Darious kicked me out," he said with a sheepish grin. "He had good right too; I was way out of line. I guess because things haven't been going well at work, I was acting like a kid."

"Yeah, I can see that," she said with a big grin.

"Now don't you start in on me!" he retorted as he kissed her hand.

"When will the kids be home?"

"About ten minutes. Can I get you some hot tea?"

"That would be great!"

Just as he sipped his first taste, the kids came tussling through the door, bringing the cold with them. Before they got across the room, the coats were off and the hats were stuffed in the sleeves. They got thrown on the nearest table as the boys hurried to sit with Elias. They had become buddies over the past few months.

Duane asked, "Momma, can I have some hot chocolate with Elias?"

"Yeah, me too!" James piped in.

"Take your coats upstairs and HANG them up. Wash your hands! Then we'll see."

Elias smiled; he loved to witness Abby with the boys. It was a sweet, savory interaction that reminded him of a distant past tucked away in his own mind, a perpetual part of life shared and treasured. He remembered what was really important for the first time in a long time.

The boys came bounding down the stairs over to Elias. Duane always sat across from him and James slid in beside him. Abby brought out the steaming hot chocolate for each one of them. A plate of cookies was placed on the table between them. The cookies were arranged on the plate like fallen dominos, overlapping in a circle. Elias marveled at the little details born out of love this woman did without realizing their impact.

"Don't you think this will spoil these boys' dinner?" he said with a false dramatic sternness in his voice.

Abby grinned at his tease. He timed his spiel just right to make the boys hesitate before grabbing a cookie. They looked at their mother and at him and realized they were being teased.

"Are you kidding? These two are eating me out of business!" she sighed with the same false drama.

She was proud of the fact that her boys were strong and growing and that she could provide for them. The boys soaked up the atmosphere (and the cookies dunked in their hot chocolate). They didn't realize moments like these were the stitches in the tapestry that would define their lives, but Elias did. It was a byproduct of his tragedy.

The boys dipped the cookies in the hot chocolate like Elias showed them and they savored the soft, warm, double-chocolate sweetness of the melting chocolate chips in the hot chocolate. The mugs were dripping beverage and cookie crumbs down the rims onto the table.

All that was left inside the cups were melted cookie crumbs and the boys tipped them up to get the last drop, tapping the bottom of the cup until they had tattooed a chocolate smiley face on their cheeks. Elias laughed out loud at the smiling faces of the boys. He grabbed his napkin and started wiping James's face while Abby worked on Duane. Their eyes met across the table briefly in a bonding moment that entwined their lives even tighter.

Elias's heart ached. He wanted desperately to tell Abby the truth. He wanted to spend the rest of his life with her, but he couldn't jeopardize the lives of her and the boys.

Elias cleaned the table as Abby went to retrieve a washcloth for the boys' faces.

"Show us a trick, Elias," begged Duane.

"Yeah, show us a trick, Elias," trumpeted James.

Elias had been doing parlor tricks for the boys and then showing them the science behind them. They didn't realize they were learning. He thought for a while and then motioned the boys to the kitchen.

"Abby, do you have any wineglasses we can use? And a pitcher of water?"

She reached into a seldom-used cabinet and brought out three tall, stemmed glasses she had stored there. She handed one to James, one to Duane, and one to Elias. She loved the way Elias took the time to interact with her boys. She had learned a thing or two also.

"Now, can we have a pitcher of water, no ice please?" Elias said in a way that would make a real magician proud, building the anticipation to a real show level.

They headed out of the kitchen back to the booth. For once, the two boys walked carefully, cradling the glasses entrusted to them so as not break them and spoil the show. Elias motioned the two boys to sit across from him and place their glasses on the table. He put his glass in the middle of the two.

"Now, if my beautiful assistant will fill the glasses equally to three-fourths of their capacity!"

Abby did so with an exaggerated flair. Elias then placed his left hand palm down on the table with the base of the glass under his index and second finger with the stem sticking out between his knuckles.

"Observe the magic of sound."

He waved his hand in a dramatic fashion and brought it down to the glass. He wet his index finger slightly and rubbed the edge of the glass until a tone sounded from the glass. The boys' eyes got big.

"Let me try!" they said in unison.

Elias spent the next few minutes teaching them how to finesse the sound out of the wineglass.

"I did it! I did it!" they said in wide-eyed wonderment almost in unison.

"Now, for our amazing finish. Duane, take a drink of the water from the magic glass. James, take two drinks from your magic glass. Now, let's repeat the experiment."

Elias patiently watched as they practiced until they got the individual tones to emit from their glasses. Then he rubbed the edge of his glass as he poured different amounts out of his glass. When the novelty wore off for the boys, he explained to them how the friction of their fingers set up the vibration in the glass and the different amounts of water caused the different tones. He wasn't sure how much they retained or even understood, but they would remember the fun and marvel at things scientific.

The boys were getting restless. Abby marched them upstairs, so they could play and watch cartoons. Elias sat absentmindedly rubbing the edge of his glass. He knew the science of the sound waves pulsating from the glass. He thought about the fact that it didn't matter what position around the glass he was, as long as he could hear it, the tone was the same. He imagined the waves as they rolled away from the source in a perfect, symmetrical pattern, invisible to the eye but beautiful to the ear.

He thought maybe he would try to find a gyroscope so he could show the boys next time about centrifugal and centripetal force. He used to play with one as a child. His grandfather had given it to him on his third birthday and shown him the wonder of the spinning top and explained to him the forces involved that kept it in perfect symmetry until the spinning slowed and it would waver and wobble to an awkward stop. Most three-year-olds wouldn't understand what made a top work, but he did. He was fascinated.

When Abby came downstairs, Elias was staring into space, motionless. His eyes were open wide, but he didn't see her when she entered the room or acknowledge her when she sat beside him. She touched his arm, and he jumped. A broad smile crossed his face slowly. He caressed her cheeks with both hands and drew her in for a long, exciting kiss. It took her by surprise. He slid out of the booth and grabbed her and danced around the floor like a mad man.

"Elias, be careful!" she admonished, giggling, "You might break something!"

He hugged her, lifting her off the floor and twirling her around. Then he gently put her down.

"Your boys might have solved a problem that has stumped me for months." His eyes danced with excitement. "I can't stay, but see if you can get Coy and Birdie to watch the boys tomorrow night. We need to go to dinner and a movie to celebrate!"

"Celebrate what?"

"Us, and the fact that we might just have made the greatest breakthrough in modern scientific history!"

He was bragging more than a little and taking a lot for granted, but sometimes the solution to a complex problem was so simple. He had a lot to do.

"I gotta go! See you tomorrow about five, ok?"

He raced out the door, leaving her shaking her head. She smiled at his impetuous behavior. There was never a dull moment with Elias. That was part of his charm. She called Coy and Birdie to make the arrangements.

Elias caught the next bus to a hobby and toy store he had noticed down the street from the clothing store he frequented. He bought some disc magnets, a gyroscope, and a regular spinning top. He caught the next bus to Dubai International and got right to work. He placed his new toys on the table in the conference room and practiced his presentation. He spent the rest of the night entering his new data into the computer simulator.

His head snapped back as he awoke from his latest catnap. He focused his eyes on the screen and started to type again. Eight o'clock and the sun was just peeking through his window. He shook away the cobwebs and checked his last data entries. He checked and double-checked his parameters and with one last stroke sent the new software to the flight simulator. He walked to the simulator room. His hand was visibly shaking when he closed the hatch and booted up the new software. The machine hummed the familiar sound as it activated the propulsion system. This was a full-sized mockup of the flying machines, but everything happened in virtual reality.

He took the control and punched in 200 meters. On the screen, the machine rose to 200 meters. The machine was stable, no sign of the wobble or catastrophic inversion that had happened so many times in the past. He rolled the control ball forward slowly. Instead of the nose dive or the unstable wobble he was used to, the simulator accelerated smoothly. He rolled the control until in virtual reality he was approaching the speed of sound. He made an abrupt left turn. The machine simulated a left turn flawlessly, the same to the right.

He shut down the machine and recorded his data. He'd been up all night working, except for a few catnaps, and should be dead tired but his adrenaline was flowing. It would be two days until he could show his findings to the other team members and that was killing him. He felt like a kid who couldn't wait for Christmas. He was floating on air as he left for home. Even though it was cold out, it was sunny, and that matched his mood. He decided to walk home.

The half hour walk in the cold weather brought him back down to earth. By the time he reached home, his energy was waning. The warmth of his apartment engulfed him. As soon as he took off his coat and hung it in the closet, his high gave way to a wonderful, relaxing, engulfing fatigue. His brain was demanding rest from the stress, and the fatigue allowed his body to go only one way, to his bed. His head fell on the pillow and his lights went out.

The signs of life started to stir in his head. It was a slow, luxurious process for a change. He didn't try to rush back into the fray but instead stared at the ceiling until the fog totally lifted. He was still amazed that the answers that had eluded him for so long were so simple. He grinned. He turned and checked the time. Three o'clock. He needed to get in the shower and get ready for his date with Abby.

What would he do without her? It seemed they were meant to be together. After he finished this project, he was going to get his own life in order and tell her who he was. First, he would have to be absolutely sure that knowing his past wouldn't put her in jeopardy.

CHAPTER 15

The Eagle Has Landed

Elias had an uneventful, relaxing weekend with Abby and the boys. He was rested and ready to show his findings to all his colleagues as soon as he could get Darious to call a meeting. He was at work earlier than usual, sitting in Darious's office drinking his first cup of coffee, idly strumming his fingers on the desk in front of him, lost in thought, when Darious walked in.

"Hey, MIT, what's up?"

"You're not going to believe what's up, Darious. I went to Abby's Friday just like you suggested and was playing with the boys, when the solution to our control problems hit me. You're not going to believe how simple it was! I need to see everyone involved in the project in a meeting ASAP. Could you arrange that?"

Darious studied Elias for a minute. He seemed more at peace and focused than he had seen him in a long time, at least since they had taken on this monumental task that threatened to swallow both of them.

"Sure, I'll get them all together for ten o'clock; that ok?"

Elias's eyes lit up and he jumped up and shook Darious's hand.

"That'd be great! See you there."

Darious smiled at Elias's youthful intensity and energy as he turned to go. He knew that eventually MIT would crack the case.

Elias went straight to the conference room to work on his presentation. He was at home in front of a computer, but he immensely disliked getting up in front of people and talking. He worked on his presentation and paced. At nine forty-five, the team started to file in. Elias made small talk with them until Darious came in to start the meeting.

"Elias requested a meeting this morning and sounded urgent, so here we are. Elias, proceed, so we can get back to work."

He got up and cleared his throat and began. He was nervous and tentative at first, but his passion and excitement trumped his nerves. "I don't have to remind you of the control problem we've had from the start of this project. Our problem has been that we have been thinking vertically and in two dimensions. We have been trying to balance an egg on the head of a pin. Let me show you what I mean. See these two magnets? We have been thinking that the forces we are dealing with are on a flat plane, when in reality they follow the curvature of the earth. Our craft fly in the controlled environment, because we have artificially created the energy waves as horizontal and vertical. Look at the monitor with me.

"See the computer-generated schematic of the magnetic force around the disc magnets? They are curved around the magnet. What happens when I put the two opposite poles together? They attract and snap together. When I put the same poles together, the repulsion is the same strength, but watch what happens. As soon as I let go of the magnet, the fields around the magnet search for equilibrium, and the magnets flip and attract. We are not taking into account the forces around the machines, just the horizontal and the vertical.

"Now turn your attention to the gyroscope in the middle of the table. When I spin the top, I create centripetal and centrifugal forces that hold the top in a predictable position until it loses enough energy that the forces around the top again exert less force than the top itself, and the top falls. Our solution is similar.

"We need to create an energy field around the machine that holds it in a predictable position. This circular wave can be created with existing technology. We pulse the wave energy around the machine. Doing so creates the same effect as the mass in motion does for the top. This creates a horizontal force field that will naturally be opposed and therefore hold the machine in place. We move the machine by weakening the strength of the force in the direction we desire to go and strengthening the repulsing field behind.

"I have created the computer simulation software using these principles. I have the data available for everyone here, but I suggest we go and test it out!"

They all sat for a while, digesting what Elias had demonstrated. Some were instantly all in and excited, but others were skeptical.

"Well, what are we waiting for? Let's go fly!" said Darious.

They all filed out to the simulator. Elias was the last one out of the room.

"Well, MIT, I knew you would pull this off eventually."

"We're not out of the woods yet! We have a lot of research and testing to do, but I know we're on the right track."

Elias picked up his toys and walked out. When he got to the simulator, he was inundated with questions. He answered each one of them and smiled at the reaction of all who took the time to fly in the simulator. They were standing in small groups arguing about the best way to control the pulses, what wavelength would be best, and all the other questions that needed to be addressed. They weren't on the same page yet, but at least they were reading the same book.

The months crept by, as the team worked on the craft. The winter held on, like winters do around the Great Lakes. By the first warm days of spring, the machines were ready to fly their maiden flights outside, away from the nest with no artificially induced force screens. This posed a unique problem. These things didn't look like regular aircraft. If they were spotted, a panic could be triggered. The craft looked like flying saucers that had been the subject of speculation about aliens from other planets for centuries.

Darious didn't want to take that chance, so he and Elias got together and devised a plan. They would truck the craft overland to a remote location out west in the desert to test them. Area 51 had been abandoned by the government over fifty years. With all the austerity moves the government had to implement in the past few years, all that guarded it now were a few cameras and some drones that had computer-controlled routes at regular intervals.

Elias knew he could take out the security long enough to get in and use the facilities for a few weeks. All he needed was a way to get the machines out there. The regular trucking companies would have to report the cargo and have a manifest and the value of the cargo, not to mention they would be tracked.

"Ok, Area 51, and you can take out the security, but how do we get the craft there?" asked Darious.

"Let me make a phone call on a secured line that isn't mine."

Darious handed him his phone. "I didn't know when I signed on to this position I'd be in such criminal company," he chided.

He knew the future of the company rested on the success of these tests. "Who are you calling?"

"An old friend," was the reply.

Elias punched in the number he had committed to memory.

"Hello?"

"This is Elias, how've you been?"

"I'm fine, but I don't know any Elias," the voice on the other end said.

It dawned on Elias he'd used the wrong name. "It's me, David. I haven't used that name since I stepped out of the car in Albuquerque."

"Wow, how are you, David? I mean Elias! I didn't think I'd ever hear from you again."

"Ha, ha, me either."

"Where are you?"

"I ended up in New Detroit, Michigan. This place is great; you should stop in sometime, like when you get off your next run. I've got a business proposal to discuss with you. I'll make it worth your while. I can't tell you much over the phone, but I'll be up front with you, it's a little shady and it involves a real rig that requires a real driver."

"So, in other words, you need me to bail you out of a jam again!"

Elias grinned, "Pretty much!"

"I'll be in northern Indiana in two days. I'll call this number when I get in and you can take me to dinner."

"Sounds good. I'll be waiting to hear from you."

He tapped the phone to end the call and gave it back to Darious.

"Who was that?"

"He's the guy whose rig I stowed away on when I fled after the explosion. If it wasn't for him, I'd probably not be here. He's the only other person who knows who I really am. We are going to take him to Robinsons when he gets here in two days, just you and me. If anyone can get us across the country with no questions asked, he can."

Elias and Darious finalized the travel plans and decided who would go with them and who would stay behind and analyze the data. The truck still had to be purchased and renovated but they wanted to have Jake Tanner be in charge of that.

Two days later, Darious got the call. Jake Tanner was in South Bend at a dispatch waiting for a load. Darious rented a self-drive so he and Elias would blend in with all the other cars on the road and went to meet him.

On the way back to New Detroit, they briefed Jake about the mission to get the birds to Area 51. When they pulled up to Envirowheels, they showed him all the trucks on the back lot that had been renovated. There were old Peterbilts, Volvos, Teslas, Mercedes, and any other brand of truck on the road lined up in rows in various states of repair. Tanner was like a kid in a candy store. He walked up and down the lot, reminiscing about how it was in the good old days when drivers were drivers.

"What do you think?" asked Elias.

"I think I done died and went to truck heaven."

"Pick out the one you think would be the best for the job."

He walked down the line until he came to an old Peterbilt. He stopped and stared. He opened the door and climbed into the cab. He checked the truck out from front to back. When he climbed down, he knew this was the one.

"I called her Patricia back in the day," he said, "I put a million miles on her before the company required us to get self-drives. Not much wrong with her that some good maintenance won't fix. They just don't make 'em like old Patty anymore."

He was reliving the old days when real men drove real trucks. What are the odds that he would ever drive this truck again?

Darious took care of the paperwork, while Elias listened to the stories about the road and Patty. When the purchase was complete, they headed to Robinsons for a great dinner. Darious and Jake hit it off from the start. Elias was glad because, except for Abby and the boys, the two of them were the closest thing he had to family he could actually associate with.

When the meal was finished, Elias filled Jake Tanner in on the project. They would take two craft to Area 51 and leave the third in the test facility. Two would fit on a regular flatbed semi. They would tarp the machines, so they couldn't be seen while in transport. Elias emphasized the need to be discreet. No one outside of the Envirowheels executives who had sold the project to them and the technicians and engineers who worked on the project knew about the machines. A handpicked few who would be in on the testing knew about the mission.

"We need to get the craft from here to Area 51. We don't want a paper trail at all and no tracking devices or satellite signals. We need someone like you who knows his way around the country and can navigate without any electronics."

"You do know that this is going to take a lot longer that you are used to? I can't drive twenty-four-seven like the self-drives. I'm going to have to take sleep breaks along the way. You also have to get by the electronic checkpoints that are now lurking at every state border. I think the electronic whiz kid can handle that if I show him the way," he grinned at Elias as he talked.

"You didn't think I was going to turn you loose with my two, very expensive babies and not join in the fun. I'll be there every step of the way, riding shotgun."

The three of them discussed the details of the mission for the next two hours before they decided to convene in the morning to finalize the details.

'I have a question for you two," said Tanner. "Most things like this have a name. Why haven't you named these birds?"

Darious looked at Elias, and Elias looked at Darious. Collectively they were a CEO of a company and a computer genius, but they didn't have the presence of mind to actually name the project. They were both dumbfounded.

"We'll bring it up in the meeting in the morning," said Darious.

"This will be my first meeting with big shots," Tanner spoke up. "Do I have to dress up or bring anything?"

"Just bring yourself, and we will take care of the coffee and doughnuts," Elias piped in.

———

Darious opened the meeting the following morning.

"Ladies and gentlemen, we are on the verge of a very exciting experiment. For the first time since the start of this project, we are ready to actually attempt to fly these birds outside our laboratory. Before we do, we need to do something we needed to do when we formed this corporation and took on the monumental task of changing the way the world flies. That is naming them! The floor is open for discussion."

The din in the room was punctuated with the occasional recognizable names such as Pegasus, Genesis, and Enterprise. Darious finally got control of the group. He hadn't had this much enthusiasm at a meeting for as long as he could remember.

"Ok! One at a time, write down your entry and submit it. We'll review each one and pick the one we can all agree on. Put your name on the entry and be ready to defend it."

They went around the room to everyone who submitted a name and brought it up before the group. Genesis, the beginning book of the Bible was a contender. The Enterprise, from *Star Trek*, an old 1960s TV program, later used in the NASA Space Shuttle program, was a possibility. The last name submitted was from an unlikely source.

Julie Burgess was a young lady who was an engineer on the project. She was fastidious in her work. She was a team player and worked well with anyone she was assigned with but preferred to stay in the background and not speak up in meetings. Darious was surprised to hear from her. She submitted the simple name, Eagle.

"If you analyze the data from the machines, you will find because of their makeup that they only have the radar print of a large bird, like an eagle. Also because they do not create an extreme amount of heat, a heat-seeking system would consider them a large bird. Again, using the data we have been provided from Mr. Montague, they will soar like an eagle."

When she had said her piece, she sat back down. Darious was impressed, and so was Elias. The room was silent for a second.

"I think that was the strongest argument that we've heard. I vote for Eagle as the code name of our project!"

When Darious finished speaking, he studied the reaction in the room and took a vote. It was almost unanimous.

"Project Eagle it is. Now let's get on to the business of getting these things tested."

The rest of the meeting was spent deciding on test procedures and logistics. Jake Tanner proposed a route for the birds to take to Area 51. They had to decide on what limits to impose on the pilots of Eagle One and Eagle Two. They didn't want to be discovered, so they decided to do all flying at night in the dark phase of the moon.

When the meeting was about to conclude, Darious turned to Julie. "We need a person on-site who is as conscientious and passionate about their work as you are. I would like to offer you the position as head of data analysis on-site with the crew, if you are able to be away from home for two weeks."

She blushed. She had wanted to go so badly. This was a dream come true, but she thought she had been passed over for the assignment.

"Yes!" was all she could manage through the excitement.

The meeting dismissed, and the people dissipated slowly, talking excitedly about the project. Not since the Wright Brothers had proved that flight was possible in 1903 had there been a development like this. This was the first craft that did not rely on air to stay aloft. The unlimited energy Tesla had talked about was about to be unleashed on humankind.

People had tried before. Some had failed. Others had succeeded but then disappeared. The energy companies couldn't let the concept of unmetered free energy get a foothold in the everyday lives of citizens. There was no way of extorting the monthly fee they charged every household in the world. The old order was on the brink of losing control and would not go quietly into the night.

The committee finalized the travel plans. The truck was ready. Elias personally handled the loading of the flatbed trailer. The technicians flew the machines by remote control onto the truck. They nestled perfectly into the travel brackets already mounted on the truck.

The front craft had a cable sticking out of it that Elias instructed the technicians to plug into the semi recharging station. Elias had modified the station to be a direct feed to the Eagle drive system. There would be no need to recharge on the trip. The Eagle would provide all the power necessary. He hadn't told Tanner yet. He was going to have a little fun at his expense.

Elias spent some downtime with Abby and the boys. Abby was a mentor now to a chef who was willing to work on Saturdays, so she was free to be with the boys and Elias. The boys enjoyed the daytrips they took to on the high-speed train to Chicago to the museums and the aquarium. They also went to the occasional baseball game to see the Tigers play.

He broke the news that he would have to be gone on business for a couple of weeks. The boys took the news harder than Abby.

"Nooo!" the boys whined, "Who's going to take us to the park next week?"

They whined so much that Abby sent them to their rooms.

When they left, she put her arms around Elias's neck and asked, "Who's going to hold me tight when you're gone?"

She looked into his eyes as she gazed up at him and smiled. He wanted to stay like this forever.

"It's only two weeks, and it's very important that I go."

He hated that he couldn't tell her about the reason and the importance of the trip. Above all, he hated that he had to keep his identity from her. He had gotten away with being Elias for almost a year now and was debating in his mind whether it was safe to disclose the circumstances that actually brought them together.

"I leave day after tomorrow. Maybe you could get Coy and Birdie to watch the boys, and we could spend Sunday together after church. We could do whatever you like; I don't care as long as it is with you."

She loved this man. If he asked her, she would marry him tomorrow. She knew his past was cloudy, but she didn't care so much anymore. He was a decent, caring, genuine man, the kind who is hard to find, and her boys adored him.

"Sure, I'll set it up for the day, if they are willing. Let's take a dinner cruise on the lake. I'll make the arrangements."

He loved her. He'd ask her to marry him, if his past would quit haunting him. He couldn't shake the feeling that being with her and the boys put them in jeopardy. They would have to flee this place and live in a remote country to be together, and then one slip could lead to disaster. He just couldn't take that chance.

CHAPTER 16

The Mission

Monday morning came too soon. He awoke thinking of Abby and the day they had together on Sunday. He didn't tell her that he was going to be the test pilot in Eagle Two. Darious had insisted on being the first pilot in Eagle One, because he was the one who had seen this project to fruition from the beginning. Who could argue the point? They were leaving early to get out of town before the traffic got heavy.

It was still dark when Jake and Elias climbed into the cab of the old Peterbilt and did a final check. The bay opened, and Tanner pulled the rig flawlessly into traffic. He was grinning from ear to ear. The old excitement was back. He felt young and alive. The open road meant something. He was the master of his own destiny again.

"Keep it at the speed limit, and don't do anything to attract attention," mothered Elias, more out of nerves than concern.

"Boy, I was doing this before you were a gleam in your daddy's eye. Just sit back and enjoy the ride. We're going to race the sunrise to Nevada!"

Elias smiled. This was going to be a great trip. He was ready with his laptop. Every time they crossed a state line, the tag on the window recorded the truck so the state could collect the energy tax and track its progress. His computer program would jam the information as soon as they cleared the windshield-tag reader. The kilometers rolled by. Elias and Jake talked about everything, as they caught up on news and gossip. Tanner was all smiles. This was on his bucket list, to actually drive a truck again before he retired. Most people didn't understand why anyone would want to drive a truck. He didn't know why people had to drink or do drugs, but it was the same obsession.

He kept looking at the battery charge gauge. It didn't seem to be moving.

"I think they forgot to look at the battery charge gauge. The thing hasn't moved since we left Detroit."

Elias was trying to keep a straight face. The first experiment they were going to conduct was the compatibility of the new energy with storage batteries and the potential of the energy produced by the Eagles. They had done laboratory tests and knew the probable results, but this was the first real-world application. He was hoping Jake was going to say something soon because he had to pee really badly, but he wanted to see his reaction when he finally realized the situation.

"I know old Patricia never had this kind of range before. I'd better stop and hook her up anyway. I don't want to be stranded in the middle of nowhere with undocumented contraband because of a faulty energy gauge."

Elias strung him on as long as he could. When they pulled into the truck stop, he confessed to Tanner what was going on.

"This is not like the infamous jerky-in-the-mouth advice! This truck, with the help of the Eagle, can travel indefinitely without recharging. Now pull into that empty space and park this thing. I have to go to the toilet bad!"

Tanner looked at him in disbelief. "That's impossible! No way!"

He was still mumbling to himself when he got back in the truck. He wasn't sure if Elias was pulling his chain or not. Surely he wouldn't jeopardize the Eagles just to get back at him for a harmless, practical joke.

It was early in the trip, so they were both gung ho and climbed back into the cab ready to go. Elias had on his poker face, so Jake couldn't read it. He pulled out with the lingering doubt of disbelief. Elias knew that sometimes the best practical joke was the truth to a disbeliever.

As the kilometers rolled by, Tanner relaxed more. The disbelief turned to astonishment. "You mean I could go anywhere in the country and not pay for energy?"

"Yep, we didn't want to have to buy energy. That leaves a footprint, and we don't want to be tracked."

Tanner was in awe at what this kid could do.

As the day wore on, the two of them settled into a travel mode. Tanner took more frequent breaks and crawled into the sleeper to rest when the sun caught up with them midafternoon and began taunting him to sleep. Elias took his catnaps when they were traveling so he could keep watch over his precious cargo. They snacked in the truck on the way. They had already made about 850 kilometers, about a third of the way, before they stopped to rest and sleep. Tanner crawled into the sleeper and went to sleep immediately.

Elias thought back. It had been almost a year since his family died in the explosion He was hoping against hope that the detectives would be able to solve the mystery. Every day, that seemed less likely. He was still gathering data on the Rothfellas, but he had been so preoccupied with his new life he hadn't looked at it for quite some time. He felt a little guilty. He still had nightmares sometimes and woke up in terror. Being back in the cab of a truck for so long, just like after the tragedy, triggered the bad memories. He got out of the cab and walked around the truck, checking the straps and the tarp. Everything seemed to be in order, so he went into the truck stop and ate.

Tanner woke about three hours later and stretched. It was more work than he remembered driving a truck. He was quite a bit younger the last time he drove. His shoulders and back would be sore tomorrow. He crawled out of the sleeper into the cab.

"Good evening, sleeping beauty."

Tanner didn't catch the significance of that statement right away. Then he remembered saying that same thing to Elias when he was David the day he stowed away in his truck. He shot a look at Elias like he remembered and got out to stretch.

"I'm going to get a bite of real food. I'll be back in a few," he said to Elias as he walked away stiffly to the truck stop restaurant. Elias stood guard. Forty-five minutes later, they were on the road again. Darkness descended. The self-drives were in line like an ant colony, and Tanner was in the procession. He drove steady at the appointed speed, so the big rig blended in with all the others. It was Elias's turn to hit the sleeper. Time and fatigue allowed him a few hours of real sleep. The hum and vibration didn't seem to bother him this time.

Darious and the rest of the crew were traveling in self-drive rental cars. They had stopped for the night at a hotel. They kept in touch by text, so they could coordinate their arrival time at Area 51.

The trip was going according to plan. The truck was actually ahead of the car caravan. Tanner was in his comfort zone now.

The kilometers faded into the rearview mirror as Elias reviewed the plan in his head.

They were going to arrive hours ahead of the crew, so they could set up camp inside one of the hangars with living quarters for the others. The truck would disappear into the largest hangar and unload by remote control. The two Eagles had all the supplies they would need.

One Eagle would be in the air all night, while the other was hooked to the power grid to provide power for the ground control. The two would be switched periodically, so data on the effects of the last flight on the ship could be gathered.

Elias would provide the security drones and cameras, with data and videos collected from their own files so no red flags would be raised.

Tanner drove all night. The morning sun painted the sky in the rearview mirrors as it kept its promise to provide a scorching hot day in late summer Colorado. They were over two-thirds of the way to their destination. Tanner pulled in to a truck stop to rest and eat. Elias joined him this time. He was actually hungry. All the snack food he had eaten was not doing the trick, and he wanted to sit in a seat that wasn't moving to eat a decent meal. They worked the kinks out and stretched as they walked. Tanner's old truck, Patricia, had performed up to the expectation that Tanner promised.

On the road again, Elias and Tanner, renewed, climbed into the rig. The journey was always easier on a full stomach and an empty bladder. They should reach Area 51 as the sun set in the west. It was all up to Tanner now.

The long trek was over. They pulled to a stop at the entrance to the abandoned Area 51, headlights off, just the occasional glow of the red brake lights in the night. Elias jumped out and grabbed his battery pack and swiftly hooked up the power to the gate. He pushed the antique button, and the gate hummed as it opened for the first time in a decade. Tanner navigated his way to the chosen hangar. There was no moon, but the stars lit the endless night sky. The legends and ghosts of the past would pale in comparison to the history that would be made here tomorrow night if all went well.

Elias texted, "The Eagle has landed!" to the rest of the group as the rig rolled into the compound. They checked the hangar access doors for electric alarms and then proceeded to cut the locks with a laser torch. Elias opened the access door and disappeared inside. He unlocked the gigantic sliding doors and shoved with all his might. The doors creaked and moaned like an abandoned cemetery gate as they reluctantly moved from their fifty-year hiatus.

Elias sneezed as fifty years of undisturbed dust swirled in confusion around his head. The rig pulled in and he fought the doors closed. Tanner turned the truck lights on, and Elias checked the perimeter of the building to make sure no light could be seen from outside. He came back breathless from his recon and gave Tanner a thumbs up.

Tanner climbed out of the cab and started the process of removing the tarps and straps that bound the Eagles. Elias chipped in and helped fold the tarps for the return trip. When the Eagles were free, Elias powered up the back one with his remote and waited for a few seconds and then gently maneuvered the machine clear of the truck and set it gently down on its own legs and opened the bay. He unplugged the cable from the truck and gently lifted the front Eagle and set it down beside its mate. Every available spot inside both craft was filled with monitoring gear and camping equipment and supplies. Everything would be done from this hangar, so they would be as inconspicuous as possible.

Tanner and Elias worked through their fatigue to set up camp. The ten-by-ten inflatable cubicles they would call home for the next two weeks were lined up facing one another, eight in all. The air pump provided filtered, climate-controlled air to ward off the extreme heat of Nevada summertime and the chill of the evening after sunset. This would ensure the comfort of the people and the integrity of the equipment involved. Portable camping latrines would have to do until daylight when Tanner would check the possibility of activating the facilities in the hangar.

The rest of the group arrived later. Elias opened the compound gate and ushered them in. One side of the hangar door opened, and the cars drove in. Then Elias shut the door. They all grabbed their gear and picked a cubicle. When the crew had settled in, Darious called an impromptu meeting.

"Tomorrow is going to be a day that will change history. Welcome to the future. Get some sleep. The next two weeks will be very hectic. Breakfast at eight." He turned to go into his cubicle.

Julie piped up, "Wow, that has to be the shortest meeting in corporate history!"

Everyone laughed, including Darious. It didn't take long for the road fatigue to put them all under.

Eight o'clock came too soon. Tanner was already up and had the coffee on. They sat around and ate their cold breakfast bars and drank the first coffee of the day and made small talk about the mission and their place in history.

Tanner was on a mission of his own. He was going to locate the nearest of the three wells that used to supply the compound with water and try to activate the old pump, so the group could have more than primitive living conditions for the next two weeks.

The door to the old pumping station creaked and groaned when Tanner finally got it to move. He wiped the dust from the old gauges and figured out how he could isolate the hangar they were in by shutting off all the valves but that one. The water tower hadn't had water in it for fifty years, but this was a military base after all. One thing the military knew how to do was overbuild things.

The only source of power with enough energy to run a pump of this size was the Eagles, or Patty. He opened the huge electric panel on the wall and studied it until he figured what to do to deactivate every circuit except the number one well pump. He followed the wires from the hangar into the main breaker and isolated the circuitry in the hangar. He maneuvered the old truck as close as he could to the huge, electrical panel and hooked a wire on the terminals to the batteries through a converter.

He made his way back to the pump house and activated the breaker. A low hum emanated from the old pump. The whole pump house vibrated as the water coursed through the pipes for the first time in fifty years. Air in the pipes made them hammer and quake. After a few minutes, the old pump settled down as the air worked its way out of the system. Gauges started telling him the story of what was happening.

Tanner smiled at the fact that the old system still had the measurements in gallons, instead of liters, per minute. The head pressure started to slowly climb as the water tank started to fill. With the pumping capacity of this pump, it wouldn't take long to fill the tank with the amount of water the crew would use during their two-week stay.

He checked the tank for any leaks. He went back to the hangar and opened the restroom and shower stalls. He got the brightest light he had with them and entered each room cautiously shining the light in every nook and cranny. He was looking for scorpions, spiders, rattlesnakes, and lizards lurking in the stalls and the showers. He'd check the drains again when the water started flowing.

It was only midmorning, and the heat was oppressive. Tanner took a cold, water bottle back with him to the pump house, rubbing the cold bottle on his forehead for some relief. The team would still have to drink bottled water, because he didn't want to take a chance on the purity of the system, and he didn't know the procedure for making it potable.

The pump had been working for about an hour. The gauges showed the number of gallons pumped and the head pressure in the tower. He let it run while he went back to the hangar and turned on the water in all the latrines and the showers. At first, it ran red with rust and sediment in the water and piping but gradually turned clear. The hot water hissed the air out of the water heater tank before it settled into a smooth flow. They were in business. He smiled at the fact that he put himself on latrine duty. He remembered when he was late for curfew in the Marines and got put on two-week latrine duty and swore he'd never do that again.

Never say never, Tanner thought.

He broke into the janitor's closet and found a stainless-steel hose and proceeded to hose off the dust and grime. He'd have this place shining in no time.

The crew had been busy arranging the equipment and checking the tracking monitors for the first flights after nightfall. By lunch, they were set up and ready. They snacked on the provisions they had brought with them and milled around the hangar until it was so hot they were delegated to the confines of the makeshift cubicles. There was nothing to do now but wait for nightfall.

Elias checked his security again to be sure the group was undetected. Darious climbed into Eagle One and went over the procedures again, although he knew everything by heart. This was like the countdown at a rocket launch in slow motion. Anticipation oozed out of every pore of the crew. Some paced like expectant parents, while others stared off into space. Nightfall could not come soon enough.

Tanner walked up to the group, refreshed and perky. "Anybody up for a nice refreshing shower?"

They all looked at one another in disbelief. They thought at first he had to be kidding.

"Men on the left and women on the right!" he said grinning from ear to ear. "I'll see if old Patty has enough energy left to cook us a nice spaghetti dinner while you all are wickedly wasting all that precious water!"

There was a mass exodus as everyone went to check out Tanner's handiwork. His sergeant would be proud of the shine on the old military facilities. Tanner grinned as he went about getting the evening meal ready. He listened to the banter as the crew readied to indulge in the simple pleasure of a shower.

A half hour later, the smell of garlic-buttered, Italian bread and the simmering spaghetti sauce wafted through the hangar, inciting the hunger of the whole crew. Tanner lined them up cafeteria style and loaded them up with the food.

"We can't make history on an empty stomach!" he chided.

They sat around and talked and laughed and swapped stories. The time seemed to creep forward a little faster. The sun was getting lower. It finally seemed to touch the mountains in the distance, setting off a firestorm of color that in itself was worth the journey from the green land of the Great Lakes to this different climate. The time was getting close.

The crew helped Tanner clean up, thanking him for the wonderful surprises. They headed to their appointed stations. Elias helped Tanner hook Eagle Two to the truck, so it would have a full charge in case something unforeseen happened. That way they could put some distance between Area 51 and home before they needed to recharge.

Darious made the call, "Launch in fifteen minutes!"

The group headed to their makeshift command center and waited, checking and rechecking the link between the machines and the computers.

When all was deemed ready, Julie said, "Let's do this."

The large hangar door was opened, and Eagle One rose at the pilot's command. Darious walked beside it out of the hangar and stopped on the tarmac. It was agreed that the first round of tests would be conducted by remote control until the machines were deemed airworthy in this new, uncontrolled environment. They were scientists, not test pilots. Maybe a little too cautious, but the idea was to find out if the craft could fly, not how high. If all went well, a pilot would be added.

Darious said a silent prayer and proceeded to follow the parameters agreed upon—200 meters straight up; then 500, left turn, right turn; 180-degree turn at seventy knots, then the same at one hundred knots. One thousand meters, and he repeated the routine flawlessly. The monitors hummed with the input as the engineers' doubts and fears dissipated. They were cheering for Darious like the crowds at the Michigan State championship games of long ago. When the first battery of tests was finished, Elias took Eagle Two and repeated the route that Eagle One took flawlessly.

After the engineers had finished analyzing the data and inspecting the machine, Darious climbed the steps to history. He hadn't had this much of an adrenaline rush since his playing days. When the ramp closed with a whoosh, and he was alone in the bird, he knelt and prayed. He prayed for safety and success, but he also praised God for giving him the opportunity to change the world! Little did he know the impact his craft would have. He was humbled by the experience.

He touched the top of the seat, and it swung around to accommodate him. He nestled in and turned the seat to the control screen. The familiar click assured him that the seat was locked in place. He fastened his harness for the ride of his life. He placed his hand on the control ball and the screen came alive. He strapped on the headset.

"Ready, Fifty-One," is all he said.

"Ready Eagle One, proceed with protocol."

He was physically shaking, though his voice was calm. He pushed on the control and the machine shot into the air, pushing him into the seat with such force it distorted his face. He managed to slide his hand off the control stopping his ascent. The machine slowed almost instantly causing the harness to strain against his considerable body mass. He could feel the blood rush to his head leaving him lightheaded and momentarily disoriented.

"Two Gs is too fast for the first time!" Fifty-One admonished.

"Sorry, Fifty-One, too much adrenaline. Control needs to be calibrated."

"Touch needs to be softer, Eagle One!"

Darious grinned. When he regained his composure, he proceeded to run through the preapproved program. Eagle One responded to every test. After an hour, he returned to the hangar.

Elias took out Eagle Two and repeated everything Eagle One did. Elias learned from the data that Eagle One provided and was a little lighter with his touch. His machine performed flawlessly.

Every test became more difficult and demanding on the machines. By the third night, it was agreed that the Eagles were worthy of carrying copilots. Not only would this help with the debriefings, but it also allowed pilots to be trained for future testing. When the Eagles got back to the nest, they would be completely torn apart and analyzed for any ill effects of the demanding flight tests performed over the two-week period.

By the last night of scheduled testing, the only person who hadn't flown was Tanner. Elias saw him watching intently from a distance and walked over to him.

"You want a ride?"

"Are you sure the thing is safe?"

"No worries! I bet my life on it."

Tanner walked up the boarding ramp reluctantly to the inside of the Eagle. Elias showed him how to swivel the seat and strap in. Elias waited to be cleared for flight and eased onto the tarmac. When he was cleared, he rose slowly, showing Tanner the controls and getting him used to flight. After a few minutes, the questions started. "How do you fly these things with absolutely no lights?" was Tanner's first question.

"We use a sonar system similar to the one that bats use to maneuver at night when they leave their caves. We use different frequencies than they do, and we have the input and output connected to a software algorithm that converts it to real-time computer images. We manually operate it with the control on the right of the cockpit chair you are sitting in, or we can put the plane on automatic pilot and it can fly the prescribed route by itself.

If I tried to run the Eagle into the side of a mountain, it would automatically override my stupidity and stay a safe distance from the obstruction according to what speed it was traveling."

"How fast will this thing fly?"

"We don't know yet. We don't want to push the envelope until we analyze the air frames from this testing. So far, we have limited it to three-hundred knots. If the structural integrity is intact, we will increase it on the next test flights. We are limited only by the strength of our engineering and, of course, by the speed of the frequency of waves we are riding on. This is all so new that we have more questions than answers."

Tanner stared at the screen, intently learning all he could. Elias rolled the control forward with a flick of his wrist, catching Tanner off guard. They accelerated with such force that Tanner was slammed into the seat like a fighter pilot for a few seconds until the Eagle reached the preset speed. As soon as the sensation stopped, Elias rolled the control left.

The Eagle went left almost instantly as the nose aligned ninety degrees left and reached speed again. There was no banking into a turn. When the Eagle was commanded to turn, it turned on a flat plane, not relying on air to redirect but instead following the centripetal/centrifugal forces, like in the Bible with David's slingshot when he hurled a stone at the giant.

Again, the force threw Tanner into his seat with his head against the side of the cockpit chair like a race car driver slamming into a turn at the Indianapolis 500!

"What's going on up there?" control demanded.

"Nothing, just a little unauthorized testing."

Elias looked at Tanner, innocently grinning with mischief.

Tanner screamed into the mic, "He's trying to kill me, that's all! You wait until I get out of here, buddy! You better be sleeping with one eye open from now on!"

Elias laughed and finally got down to the business of testing the machine. He went through the test protocol and then turned to Tanner and asked, "You want to fly the bird?"

Tanner looked at him incredulously. "I don't know how to fly."

"It's simple. Just lay your hand on the control, and I'll fly you through it until you understand."

Elias put the bird through its paces until Tanner understood the concept of the controls.

"Lay your hand on the control, like you would normally in a relaxed state. I'll punch in the protocol and pass codes to add your handprint to the memory. After we complete the process, you can practice flying for the rest of the mission."

By the end of the mission, Tanner was hooked. "How do I go about getting certified and licensed to fly one of these things?"

"The FAA doesn't know anything like this exists yet. I'm sure it will require us to produce all our test results and some kind of training procedure for pilots. We just haven't got that far in the process, so for now your handprint allows you to fly with us until we get further along in our testing. Now, let's go home and you can try your first landing."

Tanner's palms were sweating as he reached the designated coordinates.

"Punch in ten meters."

Tanner did as he was told. The craft hovered over the designated spot waiting for input.

"Gently roll the control backward."

Tanner rolled it back a little fast and the machine settled hard enough on the landing gear that it almost bounced like a grasshopper.

When it did settle, Elias looked at Tanner and calmly stated, "Any landing is a good landing if you can walk away from it." He had a twinkle in his eye.

Tanner swung the cockpit seat around and exited the bird down the ramp. He was hooked.

The last day, they packed the birds to leave. It was mentally hard to put the Eagles back into their cages for the ride home after seeing just a small part of their capabilities. It was like tethering a wild bird in Elias's mind.

At nightfall, they put black tape on all the brake lights and opened the hangar door for the last time. The airbrakes kicked dust as the truck stopped to allow Elias to climb out of the truck to shut the hangar door. The cars were already to the perimeter of Area 51, when the birds arrived. They convoyed in the starlight until they were clear of the access road and ready to enter the normal traffic of the real world. They hurriedly removed the tape on all the lights and put their temporary home in the rearview mirror.

The lights of the vehicles came on, casting a surreal shadow. Was this a pleasant dream? The whole crew settled into a hushed silence as the kilometers disappeared behind them, lost in their own thoughts, each questioning this reality. Exhaustion settled on them as the adrenaline left.

The last thing Elias remembered was normalizing the drones and the cameras, so they could once again police the abandoned Area 51 site unmolested.

CHAPTER 17

Tragedy

The crew enjoyed a week off when they returned home. They needed to decompress and debrief after their sojourn into history. Elias spent as much time with Abby and the boys as Abby could spare, but he always found himself in the lab. He was driven by his youthful impatience and his compulsive need to create and learn. He wished sometimes that he could turn it off and lead a normal, twenty-something life but that was not his lot.

The months flew by. The days grew short, and the weather became colder and unpredictable. A nasty, mid-November morning, Elias was eating his breakfast while streaming the local Hamilton County news. The wind was blowing freezing rain that the weather station promised would be snow in a few hours. He knew he would have to take the bus today, if the company was operating.

His mouth was open in anticipation of the next spoonful of cereal when he heard the newscaster mention his family name. The spoon lowered almost involuntarily back into the bowl as he stared intently at the screen. He didn't want to miss a word of the story; after all, this was why he watched every morning.

"After these messages," spoke the reporter in her matter-of-fact voice.

The commercial propaganda glowed into his space with its pixilated power of persuasion. His eyes were focused on the screen, and his ears tuned to the sound, but his brain refused to acknowledge anything. The image of the broadcaster clicked his focus back to the screen.

"In a breaking story, we just received word that the ongoing case of the explosion of the house that killed the Alonzo Browning family has been closed. The FBI ruled, after an extensive investigation, that the cause of the blast was a faulty, natural-gas regulator. Our own Stacy Woolly, on the scene at the FBI headquarters, got this exclusive interview with FBI agent Anthony Morales.

He didn't hear a word of the interview. He sat in shocked silence until the rage burst forth, and he arose with such force that his chair tumbled across the small kitchen. He proceeded to pace back and forth in front of the screen, screaming at the agent.

"You idiot! You lying lunatic! How can you stand in front of the camera and lie like that?"

His heart pounded, his face flushed, and his jugular veins throbbed, struggling to contain the blood violently pulsing out of his brain.

The news anchor came on again. "This is a breaking story. Two Hamilton County detectives were killed in an explosion in an abandoned warehouse while following an anonymous tip about a suspected drug dealer. Dan Bolker and Justin Peters were veterans of the Hamilton County detective division. They were the lead detectives in the Browning investigation until the FBI took over. We will have more details of this tragedy that happened late last night as they become available."

It clicked in his brain. The real killers were tying up loose ends. Anyone who had any information about the case was a target. He had to get to work. He needed a confidant, someone to unload on, and the only person who knew his situation in New Detroit was Darious. He grabbed his coat and headed out in the bad weather.

The newscaster continued to talk as Elias closed and locked his front door, oblivious to the fact that he'd left his computer screen on and the breakfast in the bowl, as if he just disappeared. The sidewalk crunched under his shoes from the ice melt the apartment complex maintenance crew and the city had applied to keep the surface walkable. Sleet stung his face as he hurried to the bus stop, thinking he should have called a cab.

The bus was ready to pull away as he neared, yelling and waving his arms furiously. The airbrakes hissed the bus to a stop, and the door opened just as he stepped on the untreated edge of the sidewalk. He continued out of control until his head hit the edge of the bus door.

His anger and anxiety left immediately after impact, as his brain went into survival mode. He drifted on the edge of consciousness, aware that someone was close, trying to get his attention, but try as he might, he couldn't reply.

Someone off in the distance kept loudly calling, "Mr. Montague, can you hear me? Mr. Montague! Mr. Montague!"

Who is this Montague, and why is someone so adamant about talking to him? He thought as the strands of consciousness returned.

He was free falling in a dream when reality intruded. He was Montague. He momentarily jolted awake with the realization that he would have to be careful what he said and did in his vulnerable state. As reality returned, he decided to stay unresponsive for a while, so he could gather his thoughts. He was strapped to a gurney and lofted into an ambulance. The siren wailed on the way to Henry Ford Hospital. The paramedic talked to him the whole way, trying to get a response. Concussion protocol required the medic keep the patient awake if possible. He finally had enough of the questions.

"I'm ok! Why am I in an ambulance?"

"You have a gash five centimeters long in your scalp that will require stitches, and a possible concussion," replied the medic.

Elias groaned. This was all he needed. His head was starting to hurt as the ambulance pulled in at the emergency entrance. He was unloaded and taken to a room in the ER. The doctor examined him and instructed the nurse to prep him for the stitches and draw blood for tests.

Elias was only half listening when the doctor rattled off the tests he wanted to perform, until he heard DNA. Of course, that was now standard procedure when anyone was admitted to the hospital. His stomach tied in knots. He could change his name and transfer his prints, but he couldn't change his DNA.

The doctor stitched his wound and decided because he did lose consciousness that he should stay overnight for observation. He would have the test results in the morning and evaluate Elias then to see if he could be released. The nurse put Elias in a wheelchair with his clothes and belongings in a bag on his lap and wheeled him to room 289.

The nurse and an orderly helped him into bed and put his clothes in the closet. A nurse was assigned to constantly monitor his brain waves. There were wires attached to his head and the signal was sent to a computer outside his room. She came in occasionally to check on his well-being and to make sure he didn't drift off to sleep.

Elias knew he couldn't stay here. As soon as the DNA test was analyzed, David Browning would be arrested. Although his head throbbed like someone was hitting him repeatedly with a baseball bat, he refused any pain medication. He knew he would need all his faculties if he was to escape. He studied the nurse's routine and noted the time the shift was to change. At three o'clock, just before the shift change, he gathered his belongings and went in the bathroom. He changed into his clothes and waited for the nurse to come in to check on him. He removed the bandage on his head and tried to make sure that his hair covered the wound. He was waiting when the nurse knocked on the door.

"I'm ok," he said, "just had to go."

"Next time, press the call button, so we can come and help you!"

"Ok, I will."

When she left, he opened the door and peeked out. The android at the desk scanned the hallway in a methodical manner. When it looked past the computer in the hall, he came out of his room and started programming the computer to fail. Thirty seconds was all the time he had to remove the sensors on his head and walk out of the hospital.

When the lights started flashing and the alarm started to sound, he was heading out the partition door that separated his wing from the rest of the hospital. The nurse was so intent on checking the computer, that he was in the elevator going down before she thought to check the sensors. She walked into an empty room. He'd left the light on in the bathroom, so she knocked and called his name. No answer. She peeked in and found the bathroom empty, so she walked out into the hall, looking both ways, hoping he had just decided to take a walk. She went to the front desk and announced she couldn't find the patient in room 289. All the available nurses started looking for him in other rooms. He wasn't a risk to run, as far as they knew, so no special security was implemented.

Elias was in the lobby heading for the door when he called the cab. His head hurt, and he was unsteady on his feet. The cold air hit him as soon as he walked out the front door. It made his stitches ache, so he flipped up the hood on his jacket. The hood rubbed the exposed stitches, bringing tears to his eyes. An eternity seemed to pass while he was waiting on the cab. He walked behind a van that was parked in the lot where he told the cab he would be.

The hospital went on high alert and expanded the search. Hospital security was cruising the parking lots when the cab finally pulled up. Elias fell into the cab, grateful for the heat. He punched in the address for Envirowheels and slid between the seats onto the floorboard. His head pounded from the change. The car turned out onto the street in front of the hospital, and he relaxed slightly. He called Darious.

"Are you still at work?"

"Yeah, for about a half hour, why?"

Elias told him what had happened. "I'm going to need your help. I'm on my way now. I'll be there in about a half hour. Please don't leave until I can talk to you!"

"Hey, man, I'll be here. I wouldn't leave a friend in his hour of need."

A wave of relief swept over Elias when he heard those words. He pocketed his phone.

Darious made his way to the employee entrance and waited. When the cab pulled up, Elias was in the back seat. He swiped his bit-card to pay the fare and woke Elias. He got out of the cab, disoriented and weak. Darious helped him to the entrance and almost had to drag him to the elevator before he regained full consciousness.

While Elias waited in his office gathering strength, Darious went to the first aid station and selected some bandages and numbing salve to apply to Elias's scalp. As he dressed the wound, Elias told about his mishap.

"They're testing my DNA as we speak, so in a matter of a few hours all the authorities will know who I am and will come for me. I have a plan to end this once and for all, but I need to take one of the Eagles. When I'm gone, you need to close down the research until we can find a remote location to start production. Things won't be safe for Dubai International and the Eagles when they figure out I actually financed the research. We can't let this fall into the wrong hands!"

"I've been thinking about this for a long time, Elias. I made emergency plans to move the Eagles, if the need arose. There is an abandoned silver mine in New Mexico that would fit our needs. It is isolated, and the laboratory and the Eagles can be hidden deep in the mountain. I've set up a ghost mining company and purchased it. I'll start the process of moving. We need to work on getting you out of here tonight."

"I need to see Abby and explain everything to her. She has a right to know the truth before I disappear. Could you drive me over there? I also need to stop and retrieve my computers at my apartment."

"Sure, let's go. It will be dark soon and we can get the Eagle prepped."

Elias was gaining strength. He didn't falter when he stood now, and his double vision had subsided, along with his headache. He walked to Darious's car on his own power. They stopped by his apartment to retrieve his computer gear. Soon the police would track him to his address. He wanted to make sure all his surveillance footage of the Rothfellas went with him. He called Abby, so she would be ready for him. He told her about his mishap on the phone but not of his plans. He wanted that to be face to face.

Darious waited outside as Elias went into Abby's Place. She took one look at his bandaged head and ran over to hug him. She didn't know her world was going to be rocked to its foundation in a few short moments.

"Shouldn't you be in the hospital?"

"I was, but I escaped."

"What do you mean you escaped? Nobody deliberately leaves the hospital in your condition! We've got to get you back there!"

She was frantic at the sight of his bandaged head.

"Please, sit down and listen to me. I don't have much time. I'm not Elias. My real name is David Browning. My father was Alonzo Browning."

She almost fell into the seat where they and the boys had shared so many laughs and so much love. Her eyes were glazed as her brain started to analyze what he was saying. She was finally learning what she needed to know. He told her of his flight from Indiana and about the powerful banking family who was after him.

"Abby, I couldn't let you know. Every time we were together, I always had in the back of my mind how I might be putting you and the boys in jeopardy. In my mind, they might come after you to get to me."

He continued, pacing the floor as he talked. "You have every right to tell me to leave right now and never come back. I changed my identity, but I can't change my DNA. When the test results come back, and they find out who I really am, once again I'll be a fugitive."

Tears were rolling down her face now. She knew the next words were, "I have to go and never come back." But they never came.

"Abby, I'm tired of being a fugitive. I have a plan to get the bad guys off my back, and it involves you and Darious. They will come and interrogate you and Darious and everyone they think I ever came in contact with. They will monitor your restaurant and your phone. You'll be watched night and day until they are certain you don't know anything, so I'm not going to tell you anything."

"I will be sending Darious encrypted messages every month. He'll come here around three when you are closing and order a slice of peach pie and sweet tea. Just make small talk, but don't mention my name or talk about me. That will let you know I'm ok. When I'm ready, you will get a call from me. We can talk for as long as you want. I'll be baiting the trap."

He continued. "After that, it's up to them to find me. I don't know how long that will take, but I know it won't be long. I'm going to map it out for them."

She jumped up and hugged him and kissed him all over the face with wet, salty, teary kisses. He embraced her and kissed her passionately, searing the moment into his mind. If things didn't go as he planned, this could be their last kiss.

"Can you go up and try to explain to the boys why you won't be around for a while? They will feel abandoned again if you don't," she managed through her tears.

"I couldn't leave without seeing them."

He hated the idea of not seeing the boys. They had become his family along with Abby. He took her by the hand and they both slowly climbed the stairs, dreading the task of telling the boys they wouldn't see the closest thing they had to a father for a very long time. They hesitated at the door and wiped their eyes and tried to put on a different face.

He forced a smile, as they became aware of his presence. They ran over and mauled him as they always tried to do. He scooped them both up in his arms and held on tight. They immediately sensed something was wrong. The tears flowed from Abby's eyes as she listened to him try to explain to the two young boys why he was going away.

"There are some really bad men trying to hurt me. I have to make sure that they can't do that before I can come back. I want you two to be good and take care of your mom until I can get back and take you all with me, Ok? Promise me!"

He pointed to Duane.

"I promise!" came the reluctant reply.

He pointed to James.

"I promise!" came the bewildered reply.

He grabbed them both in a bear hug and turned for the door, waving goodbye. He had to get out of there in a hurry before he completely broke down. The tears came as he thundered down the stairs out into the cold night. The shock of the cold froze the tears to his cheeks and took his breath.

He opened the car door and closed it hard in haste like a getaway from a bank robbery. Darious drove in silence to the laboratory where Elias and the Eagle would start the odyssey to freedom.

Abby and the boys huddled together in sadness. They couldn't comprehend the drama that had just transpired.

"Is he ever coming back?" questioned James.

"Yes, he is; we just don't know when," Abby reassured him and Duane, and most of all herself. In any relationship separation, no matter what the circumstances, the children are the collateral damage.

She spent the night in the boys' room. By midnight, Duane had crawled into James's bed and slipped under the covers. Abby was lying on the bed, propped up on one arm gently stroking them both. They finally drifted off to sleep, but she lingered thinking, wondering, trying to digest all that Elias, or David, had dumped on her.

If she didn't love him so much, she could let hate and bitterness creep into her heart. Why did he not tell her sooner? Didn't he trust her? It wouldn't have mattered. She knew deep down that he was trying to protect her and the boys, but right now that seemed like a lame excuse to her. Anger, sadness, and relief were all emotions fighting in her heart for control. She was mad that he hadn't confided in her, sad for the separation, and relieved to finally know the truth. Lingering doubts could now be put to rest. She would wait for him. It was not in her nature to do anything else.

Darious drove cautiously down the slushy streets. By morning, the city would be covered by the lake effect snow brought in by the northeastern storm. Self-drives had already been banned as the emergency conditions deteriorated, and no one in their right mind would be flying tonight. He turned into the Envirowheels lot and passed through security, following the familiar protocols to get to the Eagles' nest.

Elias walked over to Eagle One and touched the familiar spot to lower the access stairs. He stowed and secured his one piece of luggage, and his computer equipment in the cargo hold. The Eagles had never been tested in such bad weather conditions. It was uncertain how the hull would withstand the icing conditions that had grounded every other flying machine in the city. He walked down the loading ramp to exchange last-minute instructions with Darious.

"Promise me you will move the other Eagles and any trace of them to the silver mine as soon as possible. The people looking for me are thorough and ruthless. I know if they discover our birds, they would weaponize them. Can you imagine the consequences? They could go almost anywhere in the world on a moment's notice and deliver death and destruction in an instant faster and more efficiently than any system on earth! Promise me!"

Darious grabbed his right hand in a brotherly handshake and looked him straight in the eye, "No one, I mean no one is going to get these birds! I've got a call in to Tanner as we speak. He's the only one I trust to move the precious cargo. He will be here not long after you leave. We have already gathered all our data and equipment and loaded the flatbed with the other two birds. Any other equipment we need, we will buy. All traces of Dubai International will be gone by morning. All the technicians have been notified of the need to move and are willing to go wherever we go."

"I'm going to stay behind until the authorities are satisfied that no one knows where you are or how you got there."

"I'm going to send you an encrypted message every month. I need you to go to Abby's Place at three o'clock the next day and order a piece of peach pie and sweet tea. That will let her know I'm ok."

"I think I can handle that. Abby has the best peach pie I know of." Darious smiled to reassure Elias he was on top of everything.

Elias hesitated. He didn't want to leave. Darious sensed his separation anxiety and comforted him in guy speak.

"Go, MIT! We got this. Be sure to send me the data on how the Eagle does in this nasty weather."

With that, he let go of Elias hand and slapped him on the back. Elias knew he needed to go. He was grateful for Darious's strength.

He disappeared into the bird and turned his attention to preparing for flight. He knew the protocol by heart. The familiar hum reassured him that the Eagle was ready for the journey. The screen went through the checklist. When it asked for a destination, Elias punched in the address to the penthouse in the Dubai high-rise apartment building that the Browning Foundation owned. No one had occupied it for months.

It used to be a conference center for the foundation, but since Alonzo's untimely death a power vacuum threatened to undermine the very purpose of the benevolent organization. Alonzo thought that his oldest son, David, would be groomed for the job by the time he had to step down, a serious oversight by a usually astute leader.

Elias signaled Darious through his monitor to open the bay door. The huge overhead opened to a swirling, white-out snow. The whiteness was deceiving. Streetlights were lost in the snow. A peaceful calm permeated the city, belying the serious nature of the storm. The traffic was stilled. The TV news had only closings and perilous warnings for their audience, ideal conditions for a getaway by a wanted fugitive. The craft buffeted as it met its challenge. Elias was concerned about icing. The Eagles had never been tested in such terrible weather. Theoretically, because they had no wings and the aerodynamics that kept normal craft in the air did not apply, he should be safe.

As soon as he cleared the building, he programmed the altitude he chose for his journey. At least this time he would flee in comfort. The Eagle responded as he pressed the console control. The rapid rate of ascent caused his head to ache. He was buffeted by the winds and the extra weight the machine was struggling with as ice accumulated on its surface.

At 30,000 feet, the clouds thinned. At 40,000 feet, the clouds fell away. He wiggled the control left and right violently until he heard a strange moaning as the ice cracked and slid off the sleek hull. His brain protested the motion he created to the point of passing out. The craft smoothed out, and the computer took over as his head slumped and his hand slid off the control.

He woke to the monitor beaming the pertinent information the craft needed to operate. The direct camera feed showed the orange glow that would be a time-lapse sunrise as the earth rotated toward it and his cocoon traveled east at 600 kilometers per hour. The deep blue of the high-level atmosphere provided little deflection and distortion to the pureness of the sun's power. His isolation from humankind was complete. It would be nearly twenty hours before he reached the helipad on top of the penthouse prison he would occupy for the next few months until he could bring his plan to finality.

His heart already ached for Abby and the boys. His soul pined for the life he almost had. The stress of the day caused him to drift into a subconscious wandering. He thought of his pursuers and what they would find when they stormed his apartment. He left his TV on and the bowl of now soggy cereal on the table next to his phone. A neat package that cried, "Come and get me!" At least this accident made him realize he couldn't live his life looking over his shoulder. It was time to face his demons. He drifted into a deep exhausted REM sleep.

He awoke to stiff joints and numbness. He hadn't moved for over ten hours. He unbuckled his harness and checked the cabin pressure and the oxygen level. They were both in the normal range. The Eagle was performing flawlessly. This bird had never flown this high, this fast, or this far ever. He would have a lot of useful information for the group when he got settled in at his destination.

He was famished, so he opened the emergency storage door and found water and a military-style meal, ready to eat (MRE). It wasn't first-class airline fare, but it kept the angry down in his stomach. He stretched and moved around as much as he could in his cramped cabin, trying to shake off the stiffness. He touched the dressing on his wound gently, as if to confirm this was not a dream.

Claustrophobic boredom crept into his very being. He sat down and strapped in. The bottom corner of the screen showed him the progress he had made. He was a little over halfway there. He started tweaking the speed—700 kilometers per hour, 800; he hesitated and stopped at 900. The ship complied. He listened for changes in the noise the machine made. The only change was the muffled sound of the atmosphere being reluctantly pierced. The characteristic hum had changed pitch slightly.

The fierce battle for position, taking place just a few meters from his body between the hull of the ship and the air, was monitored by a temperature gauge sensor. It was a minus ten degrees Celsius air temp, but there would be a speed when that air friction would start to cause the hull to heat to a critical temperature. He was far from that friction, he hoped. He allowed the sensors to monitor the hull at the new speed for a half hour, while he captured the data for future reference.

His claustrophobia, his curiosity, and his youthful invincibility was stirred into an intoxicating beverage. With every gulp, inhibition fled. First, 1,000 kilometers per hour, then 1,100. At 1,200, the ship started to shudder, and he pushed the envelope forward. The ship shivered in the cold wind it was creating. At 1,300 kilometers per hour, his madness was rewarded. The ship settled into a smooth cruise, void of noise.

Over the ocean, devoid of human ears, the tiny craft had created a clap of thunder like heard after a bolt of lightning. Elias didn't hear it. He was traveling under different rules now that he had broken the sound barrier. The intoxication waned, and a big triumphant grin crossed his face. Mach one was shattered. He marveled at what Darious's machines were capable of. He knew Darious would be furious when he read the data at the foolish chances Elias had taken in the "name of science."

The monitor told Elias that he was about to cross over land, so he dialed the bird back to 600 kilometers per hour. The small craft stumbled back through the Mach speed and settled in for the last leg of the trip. The Eagle slowed and started its descent. Elias took the controls when they reached touchdown mode. The craft nestled gently onto the pad that VIPs used when meeting to determine the distribution of the wealth the Browning Foundation readily shared with the world's needy and oppressed.

Elias lowered the ramp and walked stiffly to the elevator and entered the code to operate the lock. He descended to the floor below to over-the-top opulence. Only in Dubai would someone find such unapologetic trappings of wealth. Muslims, Christians, and many other religions were present in the professions of the beliefs of Dubai residents, but their true god was wealth. They were one of the first societies to see the advantage of the blockchain and the bitcoin economy.

Elias toured his new home. He would live in isolated luxury for the next few months until he carried out his plan for freedom. He went back up to the Eagle and retrieved his computer equipment. He opened the door to the heliport hangar and stowed the Eagle inside, out of the view of any snooping drone traffic. He secured the bird and closed the hangar door. He had work to do.

He set up his computer and opened the files he needed. As soon as it was up and running, he sent a coded message to Darious.

It said, "The Eagle has landed."

Darious sighed in relief. He had every confidence in Elias's abilities, but it was still a relief to hear from him, wherever he was. At three o'clock, he would enjoy a piece of peach pie and sweet tea, so Abby would know Elias was safe.

The police from Detroit had already been there asking about Elias, only they called him David. No doubt, from now on the FBI and the police would be monitoring everything that happened in Darious's life and Abby's. The news was inundated with pictures of David, alias Elias, wanting to know of his whereabouts and offering a reward. An arrest warrant had been issued for him, and he had been placed on a high-priority FBI fugitive list. The charges against him were vague. He was an "enemy of the state."

Abby was just closing when she saw Darious walk through the door, shaking off the cold and removing his coat. The diners were finishing their meals, and she was helping tidy up and prepare the area for the next day.

"We're closing, sir," she said as he approached, "but if you will give me a minute, I'll see that you are helped."

The last customer got up to leave as she showed Darious to the table where Elias always sat. He pretended to look over the menu as she settled up with the last patron. She hurried over to Darious in anticipation. Darious smiled and said the words she longed to hear.

"I think I'll just have a piece of peach pie and sweet tea."

A wave of relief swept over her. "Coming right up!"

She almost ran into the kitchen to fill his order. Her hands were visibly shaking as she poured the tea. She had to stop for a second and regain her composure. She hadn't slept well since Elias left. The police had been there questioning her about her involvement with Elias, but they called him David.

Darious and Abby knew they were being watched, so they were careful to not mention Elias in the conversation. Just the two of them in the same place raised suspicion.

—⟋⟍—

Elias went about setting in motion his plan of emancipation. The contractor he commissioned to build him a bomb shelter in his bedroom thought he was an eccentric, spoiled, reclusive billionaire. Maybe he was. He insisted on a reinforced concrete wall surrounded by a wall of corrugated steel designed to collapse as it absorbed a tremendous force, such as a bomb blast, surrounded by another reinforced concrete wall. His bedroom, work station, kitchen, and bathroom were now all encased in a concrete bunker that could double as a bank vault. He lined the exterior with a solid sheet of lead to deter the sensors he knew would sniff him out.

The months went by as he prepared. In the master suite, he placed an android whose only function was to be his twin. It was programmed to go to bed at the proper time and get up and move around the penthouse as he would be expected to move. It had his same body mass and same body temperature. When profiled by infrared or temperature probes, it looked like him. He called it David.

He had one more thing to do before he set his plan in motion. He had studied all the data he had gathered on the Rothfellas. To make sure he could count on them to find him, he was going to punch them where it hurt the most. just like they had done to him.

He was planning the biggest transfer of wealth in the history of humankind. One trillion bitcoin was about to disappear from the Rothfellas' coffers. Their reign of power was about to end. He didn't want any of it. To him it was blood money. Instead, every contributor to any charity who helped the oppressed around the world was going to get a windfall in their bitcoin account. He would sign the withdrawal David Alonzo Browning! The blockchain the Rothfellas were using would crumble.

CHAPTER 18

Dubai

He was standing on his balcony. He was wrestling with the moral consequences of his actions the day before. With the click of a mouse, he had taken down the powerful Rothfellas empire. The vengeance he thought would be sweet on his lips turned to bitter bile in his stomach. His family was still dead. His heart dripped bitterness from his self-imposed exile and virtual solitary confinement. He missed Abby so much she occupied his every thought. He couldn't shake the thought that he had just aligned with the devil. The line that separated him from them had blurred.

He walked back inside. Android David was watching TV. Elias conversed with him like he was a houseguest now. If anyone could hear his banter, they would think him insane, but it was the only interaction he had. He hadn't been outside his penthouse since he arrived and had to go to the lobby and replace his bit-card so his actions couldn't be traced, but that was about to change. He had to get a phone, so he could implement the rest of his plan. All his other supplies had been ordered on his computer and delivered to his door. His time here was growing short. He wanted to do this in person. The directory indicated there was a store on the second floor that could accommodate him.

He stepped into the elevator and pushed the second-floor button. Swiftly, silently, he was whisked away from his purgatory. In no time, he was standing in a spacious mall area. If he so chose, he would never have to leave this building the rest of his life. Everything he needed to live comfortably was here. He marveled as he strolled slowly to the electronics store. The smells and the sights titillated his senses. He'd forgotten how it was among the living. He might as well have been in a coma the past few months.

He bought the cheapest phone the store had and opted for the month-to-month lease. He knew the phone would be destroyed shortly. He paid for it with his old bit-card. The one he knew could be traced. The time was near. Soon he would hear Abby's voice for the first time since he'd left. He lingered for a while, just taking in other humans before he entered the elevator and ascended to his prison.

As soon as he reached his door, he calculated the time change difference. He would wait until it was five in the morning in Dubai, so it would be eight o'clock at night there. The boys would be ready for bed but still awake, so maybe he could talk to them also. That would be perfect.

After spending a restless night, trying to sleep, the alarm finally woke him just before five. He trembled as he entered her number. The phone seemed to ring for an eternity before she finally answered.

"Abby's Place!" she answered, still on work time.

"Elias's place!" he answered.

She almost dropped the phone.

"Is . . . it . . . really you?" she asked through her tears.

"Yes, it's me!"

She thought of a million things that she'd wanted to say to him in the past few months. But now, when he finally called, at this moment she couldn't think of a single one.

"Are you still there?"

"Yes! Yes! Yes!"

He felt the excitement in her voice, and tears streamed down his face.

"You don't know how good it is to finally hear your voice! I've thought of you constantly since I left."

"Yes, me too!"

She was finally regaining her composure. "Where are you? Can I ask?"

"Sure, I'm in Dubai, the United Arab Emirates in a penthouse owned by the Browning Foundation."

He figured that her phone had been tapped, so he wanted to make sure the listener knew his exact whereabouts.

"A penthouse? So, you've been living the life of luxury while I've been here struggling to make ends meet." She proceeded to tell him how after he left the government had confiscated her restaurant, and she was just an employee in her own place.

"They said I was making too much money. The TV channels have been inundated with propaganda saying the government was behind the restoration of New Detroit and the Browning Foundation was a fraud and that you would be caught and prosecuted to the fullest extent of the law."

"Doesn't surprise me, I didn't think the socialist government would let a free and prosperous society coexist in the same environment."

"How are the boys?"

"They miss you terribly. Duane has been acting up in school, and James seems to be lost sometimes. He carries on a conversation with you sometimes, just like you are still here."

"Can I talk to them?"

"They are still up; let me get them."

"Say hi, Duane."

The only time he got to talk on the phone was when Grandma called.

"Hi, Grandma."

"I'm not Grandma, this is Elias."

His eyes got big, "Hey, Jimmie, it's Elias!"

"When are you coming back?"

"Soon, I hope. Hey, I hear you're having some trouble in school."

Duane squirmed a little as he answered, "Yeah, a kid hit my friend, and I hit the kid back for him and I got caught."

"Yeah, that happens. You gotta be careful and not hit people. That's never a good thing."

He handed the phone back to his mom with a big grin on his face.

"Here's James."

"Hi, James, how have you been?"

"Fine."

"How are you doing in school?"

"Fine."

"Are you behaving yourself and minding your mother?"

"Yes"

With that, he handed the phone to his mother and bounded out of the room, leaving Elias and Abby to reconnect. They talked for over an hour about everything and nothing, imagining that they were at Robinsons, sitting across from each other holding hands. Elias finally mentioned that Abby had to get up in the morning, so maybe he should hang up. She reluctantly agreed, and they said their goodbyes. She checked on the boys and danced into her room, caressing the phone to her bosom. She slept like a baby.

The FBI had been monitoring this woman's phone for months. The only calls she ever made were to her food suppliers and her mother. Tonight, they hit the jackpot. They traced the call to the city of Dubai in the United Arab Emirates. The subject, David Browning, aka Elias Montague, had even given the location in his phone conversation. As soon as they hung up, the agent on duty at FBI headquarters sent the new information up the chain of command. The director immediately made a phone call. He conversed quietly for a minute with the shadow on the other end.

"Should I call the cleanup committee?"

"Consider it done."

He ended the call and poured himself a congratulatory drink. By week's end, one of the most embarrassing snafus of his career would be rectified. He downed the drink and sauntered off to bed.

In a few days, David Browning would be gone and all assets of the Browning Foundation would be officially confiscated by the People's Democratic Socialist party. Of course, the party wouldn't miss the few million bitcoin that would be deposited into his account, and the few party members' accounts who needed to be duly compensated.

The hardest part of Elias's plan was still to come; the wait. It was now up to forces out of his control to react. He hoped someone had taken the bait. He monitored the airspace around the building for movement, but he wasn't sure how much time he would have to react when the killer arrived. He would be in his self-imposed solitary confinement in his bunker.

Days passed. The only time he came out of his bunker was to phone Abby. An oversight on his part was that the lead lining, which kept out the surveillance of the drones, prevented phone signals from getting in or out. He sat in a chair in the doorway with the back leaned against the doorjamb with the phone in the ear that was outside the bunker. He was sitting in this fashion with his feet propped on the opposite doorjamb when the alarms screamed.

"Gotta go!" he said into the phone.

He fell out of the chair into the bunker, rolling on the floor and getting to his feet instantly. He gave the chair a Kung Fu kick out of the bunker and immediately started tugging on the heavy vault door. The phone tumbled outside the door. It was still connected.

He dove under his bed that was designed to withstand many tons of downward force, just in case. The floor moved downward and then violently back up as the blast expanded its devastation. He bounced between the floor and the bottom of the bed like a rag doll. The building belched fire out of every opening on his floor. The ceiling rose to accommodate the blast and settled back to a new normal. The view the drone saw from outside resembled a fire-breathing dragon as the intense pressure within equalized. The last thing he remembered was the interior concrete ceiling crumbling and the walls moving.

"Elias! Elias! Elias!" She shouted into the phone.

All she heard was the sound of the phone bouncing on the floor and then a hissing whump and silence. She fell to her knees with the phone cradled in her hand. She redialed to a busy signal. She caressed the phone and rocked back and forth with grief. She sensed foreboding disaster.

CHAPTER 19

Technology Failure

He drifted in and out of consciousness as the oxygen dissipated. His brain went into self-preservation mode from the pummeling. The building went from extreme pressure to a vacuum as the force of the blast gained momentum and tried to suck out every bit of atmosphere as it rushed out of every fissure it had created. Finally, the structure took air like a drowning person breaking the confines of a watery grave.

Elias was neither here nor there. He drifted in a limbo he could not understand. His body would not respond. He was paralyzed and trapped by the debris. His engineering and his technology had failed him. He lay helpless. He heard his father's voice in the distant recesses of his mind.

"Pray, my son."

The air conditioning was destroyed in the blast. The temperature outside the penthouse was 110 degrees. The blast had heated the concrete to the point it was untouchable. It radiated the heat back into his space, making the air unbearable in his nostrils.

He prayed, "God of my father, please forgive me! I thought I could live my life on my own, but I am weak. I cannot go on by myself!"

He felt himself rising from the deadly sauna into a cool, intense light. A peace flooded over him like he had never felt. Waiting for him at the end of his journey stood a robed figure with outstretched arms. Their eyes met momentarily, and Elias fell prostrate on the ground. Elias's very soul was seared by the intense love he saw in the stranger's eyes. He was unworthy to stand in his presence. He knew immediately who Jesus was. He couldn't speak, he could only listen.

"David, the one called Elias, why do you reject me?"

Lord Jesus, I believe in you! Elias thought.

"Satan and his angels believe," he replied. "That is not what I asked. Why do you reject me? You cannot serve two masters."

Matthew 6:24. No man can serve two masters: for either he will hate the one, and love the other; or else he will hold to the one, and despise the other. Ye cannot serve God and mammon, Elias thought without speaking.

"You are correct in your thinking. Your master is not me; it is technology. I protected you when they came for your family, yet you chose technology.

"I blinded the eyes of your pursuers as you fled in the fields, yet you chose technology.

"I put my servant Jackson Tanner in your path to protect you as you fled, yet you chose technology.

"I steered you on a path that would show you the greatness of your father's vision and gave you Abby to complete you, but in your youthful arrogance and self-importance you chose technology.

"Your father was the subject of their destruction. The one you destroyed was not the enemy you seek.

"Your own government sought to destroy your father's vision by destroying his whole family, including you, so it could claim his success as its own."

Elias again fell prostrate. He could barely comprehend his blindness to the truth. "Forgive me, Lord, for I have sinned greatly!"

"Rise, my son, it is not your time. You must return and be made whole and receive the Holy Spirit. Our father has a great commission for you.

"My second reign is near. The earth rumbles and quakes in anticipation. You will receive visions in the darkness. You must obey.

"Our father has chosen you among his created ones to ease the suffering of the faithful in the terrible times humankind has wrought upon itself through disobedience."

Elias came to. His nose was bleeding profusely, and he was deaf, although he didn't realize it right away. He lay stunned for what seemed to him an eternity. Bit by bit, he regained consciousness, like a computer recovering after a power outage. His eyes slowly focused through the settling dust to chunks of concrete strewn like boulders on a volcano. When he was fully conscious, he tried once again to free himself to no avail. He was puzzled. Was the dream he seemed to remember a reality or a figment of his mind? He felt a peace like he had never known. He thought of his time in New Detroit and the attitude that so puzzled him, and he understood.

The building seemed to settle, as the stones imprisoning him rolled away. In a moment, he was free. He said a silent prayer to his father, God, and to his savior, Jesus Christ. He didn't know how long he had been unconscious, so a sense of urgency overwhelmed him. He crawled out of his would-be grave and slowly rose to his feet. When he found that everything worked properly he moved to the exit stairs leading to the roof. He hoped that the way was clear after the blast.

He made his way to the roof and to the Eagle he had stashed in the hangar so many months ago. The helipad was leaning at a peculiar angle. He tried the hangar door, but the power was out. He unhooked the automatic door opener and began cranking the manual override. His body ached from the bruising blast, and his clothes were drenched from sweat as the intense sun relentlessly baked him, oblivious and uncaring of his plight. When the door was moved away enough for the Eagle to escape, he hobbled over and placed his hand on the underneath and the hatch lowered, beckoning him to freedom.

According to the dust around the landing gear, the bird had been moved almost a meter to one side in the blast, but the ship didn't seem to be damaged. He climbed into the bowels of the bird and swiveled the seat around and fell in. As the seat swung around, he fastened his harness and said a prayer to his new master. He touched the screen and the bird awoke.

As the Eagle went through the preflight checklist, he contemplated his next and last move in Dubai. He slowly moved the Eagle out of its nest and manually piloted the bird slowly away from the damaged building, looking for the drone that he knew was responsible for his "demise." When he was satisfied that it was not lurking around the building, he maneuvered the craft a safe distance away and programmed his screen. The same oxygen tanks that had kept him alive after the blast were going to serve a different purpose now. He pushed the last fail-safe he had built into the system, and the explosive incendiary bombs he had placed strategically around the entire penthouse erupted. The roof raised as the bombs, aided by the oxygen, belched its destruction. The flames seemed to rival the intensity of the sun.

What was left of the roof imploded as the structural steel melted. He said a mental "goodbye" to his android companion, David. The investigators would find nothing but black carbon. He would be officially dead to his pursuers, based solely on the reconnaissance of the drone surveillance. RIP, David, the one they call Elias.

The whole building swayed from the impact. When the aftermath of the blast dissipated, he programmed the address of the silver mine in New Mexico, a place he had never seen but one he would call home, and settled in for the journey. Once again he was starting over but armed with the knowledge that he was not alone. He prayed.

With the course and altitude set, the bird headed for home. He sent an encrypted message to Darious. "I'm coming home. Regardless of what you hear on the news, I am fine. Please contact Abby and let her know."

Darious had moved to the compound in New Mexico with his wife. They had, along with the other people involved in the Eagle's research, made a life inside the mountain. When he got the encryption, he let out a big yell. He explained to the crew that Elias was ok and coming home. He would have time to hop into the Eagle and have a nice dinner in New Detroit with his wife and then have dessert at Abby's before Elias got home.

They had been busy in Elias's absence. The two Eagles were now fitted with a new skin on the hull. The computer algorithms that Julie created allowed the ships to image their surroundings and project them like a chameleon, when they didn't want to be detected, on the hull of the ship. The system worked so well that they no longer needed to be clandestine night creatures.

"Florinda, would you please make reservations at Robinsons for lunch for two? We're about to take a road trip!"

She couldn't contain her excitement. She would follow Darious anywhere, but she had always lived in the city. She threw her energy into getting the old company mining houses upgraded into very comfortable accommodations for the whole crew. Still though, she missed the hustle and bustle, the lights, and the atmosphere of her lifetime home. It was very quiet and peaceful here, and dark! This was a pleasant surprise.

Darious felt her loneliness sometimes, even though she never complained. Maybe she could even get some shopping in before they had to get back. He readied for the trip. They would land on the roof of the old Envirowheels building. Even though the government had taken over the business, the codes he had were still good. He could get into the building through the maintenance elevator and exit to the street. They would take a self-drive to the restaurant, then shopping, and on to Abby's Place.

Abby suffered through the routine motions of her life after she lost contact with Elias a few hours ago. She tried to smile for the boys as she readied them for school. She had cried herself to sleep the night before, worrying, not knowing his fate. The news this morning had ripped her heart out.

The newscaster said—in the matter-of-fact voice she had been taught by the state, in her official uniform that was a constant reminder to everyone in New Detroit of their new reality— "Enemy of the state and fugitive from justice David Browning was located last evening in a penthouse apartment in Dubai, United Arab Emirates. With the cooperation of local government officials, according to the FBI, the floor was isolated, but he refused to surrender to authorities. An explosion shook the building, destroying the top floor. At this time, it is presumed that David Alonzo Browning perished in blast. We will have more as the investigation continues."

Abby was in a stupor. She went to work as usual. Her motions were rote. Orders came in and she filled them without any recollection of ever having done so. Many of the orders were returned for correction. The government-appointed supervisor who usually parked at the checkout came in and threatened Abby, but she gazed right through her, unaware.

Her agonizing morning faded into early afternoon in seemingly endless torture. At five minutes until three, Darious and Florinda walked in the door. Darious was loaded with the packages Florinda had purchased. It seemed she had bought something for everyone back at the silver mine.

Abby walked out slowly to help get the tables ready for the next day. In her state of mind, she didn't recognize the man and woman standing in the entrance.

"We're closing in five minutes. We can't seat you," the comrade cashier glared, devoid of compassion or respect.

"We just came in for a piece of Abby's peach pie," Darious reasoned.

Comrade slid off the stool she occupied ninety-five percent of the time and walked around the counter. She was going to make sure this big black man knew who was in charge.

When Abby recognized Darious's voice, her knees went weak. She grabbed the edge of the nearest table to keep from fainting.

Comrade confronted Darious and repeated her command. "We're closing! We can't serve you!"

Abby recovered enough to glide in behind Comrade.

"I'll stay and take care of them; they're friends of mine," she said in her most subservient voice.

Comrade swung around and confronted Abby. She hesitated, trying to think of a reason she should deny Abby's request. She ultimately thought of the revenue and leaned in to Abby as a drill sergeant would.

"I'm leaving. It's closing time but if you want to stay on and let these people stay, then I'd better see the bitcoin in the computer for the pie in the morning!"

With that, she turned and brushed Florinda aside and went for the door. Abby made sure the door was locked behind her.

"Right this way," Abby said in a way to clue Darious that the place could still have listening devices imbedded.

They followed her to the familiar booth and slid in. Darious positioned his packages in the seat beside him as Florinda slid in on the opposite side. Abby hesitated, then asked, wanting to hear the right words, but bracing for the worst.

"What can I get for you today?"

Darious was grinning from ear to ear as he said, "I'll have sweet tea and a slice of peach pie."

"And I'll have the same," chimed Florinda.

Abby visibly wilted. Darious caught her petite hand in his large one and put his other hand over hers. Her hand disappeared past the wrist. Florinda did the same. They were both afraid she might faint.

Time was irrelevant. Abby allowed the hope she had denied herself to flood her soul, dissipating the cloud of grief that had engulfed her. They stayed connected, all feeding on the energy of the power of touch that people rarely experience in this modern society. The love was palpable, engulfing, healing, bonding.

At the proper moment, Darious gently released his hand, slowly, as one would do a baby taking its first steps, not fully relinquishing until he was sure she was stable. Abby straightened and left to bring the order. She had been constantly praying for Elias's safety since he left. She grabbed the edge of the counter for support and thanked God for his mercy.

CHAPTER 20

Salvation

Elias set his airspeed at 1,100 kilometers per hour and tried to relax, but the explosions had triggered unpleasant memories that were buried deep in his brain. He prayed for his lost family and for the family he would reunite with as soon as he could.

He contemplated the events leading up to his escape. The dream, if that was what it was, of his meeting with Jesus was so real and vivid in his mind that it changed his outlook on everything. He had a new purpose and a new peace that permeated even his unpleasant memories. He was going home.

—∞—

When they were sure Abby was all right, Darious called a taxi to take them back to Envirowheels. He and Florinda started the journey back to the compound in New Mexico. He wanted to be there to greet Elias when he got home.

Abby's boys clamored in the door. Abby grabbed them both and held them tight before she herded them upstairs. She thanked God with every step as she followed. She was exhausted but content in the knowledge that Elias was on his way back to them.

The Eagle found its way to its new nest. Elias slept most of the way back, his body recuperating from his ordeal.

Darious and Florinda returned from Detroit and settled in to wait for him.

The monitors in the compound saw his progress by monitoring his sonar guidance system. When his landing was imminent, they gathered in the landing area to greet him. The Eagle landed on its own. The boarding ramp lowered. Elias hobbled down the ramp and collapsed toward Darious, who caught him and steadied him as one of the stunned onlookers ran to get a stretcher out of the infirmary.

Elias looked like he'd wrestled with a grizzly bear and lost. He had multiple bruises and contusions all over his body, and he was covered with grime from head to toe. The high of his escape adrenaline dissipated into a hypoglycemic helplessness. He needed food, water, rest, and Abby.

"Welcome back to the living. By the way, you look terrible," Darious chided with the biggest grin as he grabbed Elias's hand in the thumb-lock handshake men use to convey feelings.

Elias could only smile weakly.

"Florinda will fix you right up. As you can see, she's a great cook."

Darious sat beside his bed as Florinda prepared some quick energy food for Elias to hold him until she could prepare a full meal. Elias ate slowly with Darious cheering him on. He seemed to gain a little strength with every bite. By the time Florinda returned, he was sitting in anticipation. He ate ravenously, washing everything down with sweet tea.

"Would you like some dessert, Elias?"

He looked at her with a puzzled look and said, "Huh?"

He could hear Darious booming voice even though he seemed to be muffled like Elias was wearing ear muffs, but Florinda's softer, higher tone of voice was garbled. He looked up at her puzzled.

"Would you like some dessert?" she repeated louder.

He just nodded. She returned with a piece of peach pie and slid it in front of him. His stunned, questioning look brought a smile to Florinda's face.

She answered before he asked. "Yes, it's Abby's famous peach pie! We were there earlier today to let her know you were ok, and she insisted we bring you some to tide you over."

He caressed the dish as if it held the most precious thing in the world. Tears streamed down his cheeks when he picked up his fork and broke off just a little tip of the wedge and put it in his mouth. He rolled it around with his tongue, letting it melt slowly. He closed his eyes and saw Abby's face in his mind. Just knowing she had created this savory delight, had actually touched it, and had baked in her very essence overwhelmed him.

Florinda glanced at her big, intimidating, commanding man and caught him wiping a tear. She had to leave the room.

When Elias finished his pie, Darious jumped up and said, "Come on, man, we gotta get you cleaned up."

He helped Elias to his feet and moved him slowly to the shower, grabbing a towel and washcloth on the way.

Darious let go of Elias's arm and asked, "You got this?"

"Yeah, I'm good."

Darious left the room and Elias prepared to shower. The gentle water cascading down his body made sure he was aware of the damage he had inflicted. Abrasions burned from the intrusive water, and the bruises stung with a thousand, tiny needles. He gently lathered the cloth and patted the wounds clean. The shower base resembled a coal miner's runoff, as the filth left his body.

Darious stood outside the shower door, listening for any sign that Elias was in trouble. He was becoming a mother hen. He smiled at the thought.

Elias dressed in the robe provided and opened the door to find Darious lurking on the other side. He escorted Elias to the bedroom he would call home. Elias was sitting on the edge of the bed when Nick Harlow, one of the technicians walked in.

"You remember Nick?"

"Yeah. How are you, Nick?"

"Nick was a medic in the desert wars and he does double duty as our infirmary nurse. I've asked him to check you out."

Darious said it in such a way that Elias knew he didn't have a choice in the matter. Nick went about examining Elias. When he was done he turned to Darious and said, "He's going to be one sore puppy for a while. Those wounds are going to scab over and cause him a lot of grief. Keep him hydrated and use some of the bacterial salve in the infirmary to keep the scabs softened until they slough off. He doesn't have any deep wounds, but we need to monitor him for a few days for infection. Give him a couple of aspirin and send him to bed."

The examination was more for Darious's benefit than Elias's.

"You heard the man! Get some rest."

Elias complied. As soon as his head hit the pillow, he was out.

"Thanks, Nick."

"Hey, that's what I'm here for."

The two men left the room and shut the door. Elias was unaware.

Darious got up and dressed in the middle of the night.

"Where are you going?" asked Florinda.

"Gotta go check on the boy."

She rolled over and smiled to herself. Her big, intimidating CEO had a gentle side that not many people witnessed. She knew; that's why she loved him so. She knew he wouldn't be back to bed. Contentment filled her soul as she drifted off.

Elias woke slowly. When he opened his eyes, there was Darious asleep in the chair at the foot of his bed. He moaned involuntarily as he sat up, waking Darious with a start.

"How're you doing today?"

"I was doing great until the first thing I saw was your ugly face!"

Elias said it with a grin, until his face felt like it was going to crack. Darious got up and glared at him until a smile graced his face. He knew now that Elias was going to be ok.

"Some of the techs who are your size donated some clothes for you to wear. Yours were trash. Breakfast is in a half hour. Be there."

"Yes, sir!"

Darious walked out of Elias's room so he could dress. Later, Elias made his way to breakfast. Florinda hovered over the both of them as she served them. Elias talked nonstop about his time away, about Abby, and about the progress the team had made on the Project Eagle research. Darious filled him in, between bites. This was the first time in months that Elias had enjoyed company as he ate.

He thanked Florinda for the wonderful breakfast and excused himself. He was still weak from his ordeal, so he made his way back to bed. He didn't feel mentally up to getting back into the research mode just yet. He had deeper things to contemplate in his mind. When he rose from his nap, he walked outside to bright sunlight. He breathed in deeply of the outside air. He walked in solitude and prayer, grateful, just grateful.

—◠◠—

The second day, he was feeling much stronger. He asked Darious to walk with him. He needed to tell someone about the ordeal and the out-of-body dream he had.

"Darious, I answer to a higher power now. I can't explain it, because I don't fully understand it yet myself."

He proceeded to talk about the out-of-body experience. Darious understood the kid didn't need his advice, only his ear, so he nodded. They walked for an hour as Elias recounted his recent past.

Finally, he asked, "Darious, where do I go from here?"

"You need to get baptized and receive the Holy Spirit. He will guide you and take you as far as your obedience and your faith allow."

Elias contemplated his answer in long silence. He already knew the answer, but for some reason he needed to hear it from Darious.

Days passed.

"It's time I went home to New Detroit to see Abby. I'm strong enough now if I take it easy."

Darious nodded. "I think you're right."

"I need to brief you on the improvements we've made in the Eagles. We haven't retrofitted your Eagle yet, so you need to take

Eagle Two, your first craft. Julie came up with a new system that cloaks the Eagle so well that no one can detect its presence from fifty meters or more. We went to New Detroit to see Abby when you called, and no one was aware of our presence."

He filled Elias in on the limitations and the cautions associated with the new system. He suggested Elias take the same route that he had days before. The maintenance elevator codes could be breached easy enough to get him safely into the city to Abby's Place.

Tomorrow was Sunday and Elias wanted to get to Abby's. He needed to talk to Pastor Richard about a lot of things.

Five thirty in the morning, Elias was up and ready. As he walked out to the Eagle, he saw Darious standing by the bird, waiting.

"What happened to your beard and hair?"

"I've decided to not hide behind a beard or a different color of hair. I am who I am. I was told in my dream that God has a great commission for me, and I have faith that he will keep me safe from harm."

Darious looked at him for a minute and nodded.

"Be careful, and don't get caught. Things are different than when you left. It seems all windows have eyes and all lampposts have ears."

"And by the way, MIT, keep it under Mach one. We don't need to shatter windows and wreak havoc just because some young pup feels the need for speed!"

Busted! Elias grinned sheepishly like a kid caught with his hand in the cookie jar.

"Ok."

He disappeared into the craft and settled in as the preflight check began. When the green light came on, he lifted effortlessly into the predawn sky. In an instant, he was on his way east to meet the sunrise.

Darious said a prayer under his breath for Elias.

Elias settled in on the rooftop of Envirowheels and made his way down the elevator to the street. The sidewalk was almost deserted on this early Sunday morning. He made his way to the bus stop in the front of the building and waited. He could actually hear the birds singing in the trees. He thanked God his hearing was slowly returning as he healed.

The bus took him over the familiar streets toward Abby's Place. The friendly joy he was used to was gone. The few people who rode this early bus kept to themselves and didn't acknowledge him when he said hi. He was puzzled.

He exited a few blocks early to see if he could get something to eat at the fast-food restaurant. The people had all been replaced by robots. He ordered and swiped his bit-card. The food came out of a chute in a few minutes and was mechanically pushed toward him. The place was devoid of any character or warmth.

He walked out of the place and ate on the way. It was too depressing to eat inside, surrounded by impersonal steel machines. He threw the litter in the trash container when he was finished eating but it was overflowing and spilling its contents onto the street.

He had butterflies in his stomach as he approached Abby's door. How would she receive him after all he had put her through? The roller coaster highs and lows that had been his life had to have taken a toll on her and the kids. She even thought he was dead at one time. Still, she sent him some pie. He didn't realize how insecure he could be until Abby!

He started to knock and thought better of it. He would just lean against the lamppost until she and the boys came out.

At five minutes after nine, she appeared with the boys close behind. She was intent on locking the door and didn't notice the stranger leaning against the lamppost down the way. She turned and caught sight of him and instinctively pulled the boys behind her.

"Abby, it's me, Elias," he said straightening up with outstretched arms, palms out.

She recognized his voice but couldn't believe the change in him. She thought this day would never come. She melted into his outstretched arms without saying a word. The boys hesitated until the spark of recognition tendered explosive squeals of delight as they danced around the intertwined couple. They were both beyond tears. They savored the moment that neither was sure would ever happen.

The moment passed. They strolled leisurely toward the church, side by side, arms around each other's waist not daring to let go. She leaned her head on his chest. They moved in silence. The boys march-danced around them with the wonderful, chaotic, joyful energy only children share.

She was worried about his safety when she spoke, "We have to sign a register when we attend church. The government uses it to extort more money. We have to pay a fee to attend. Sometimes if we resist, the officials use it to declare that we are insane. Many members have had their houses confiscated and have disappeared without a trace."

"Pastor Richard has to submit his sermons two weeks ahead of time, so they can be reviewed by a committee for proper content. He also has to pay a fee for every sermon."

Elias walked in silence trying to digest what Abby shared.

"We only have a handful of loyal people who attend church regularly. I'm afraid that we will have to close our doors soon."

"I was looking forward to sitting in church with you, like we used to. I still remember the first time, when I saw my father preach in that hologram for the last time. It was like God was giving me a chance to say goodbye."

They walked on in silence, until Elias abruptly stopped and turned to face Abby.

"I need to see Pastor Richard. I have so many questions for him, but I can't sign my name on anything. The government thinks I'm dead and I need to keep it that way. But I need to be baptized."

She smiled for the first time and hugged him. They continued walking.

"My boys are the only children who attend now, so I teach the Sunday school class. I will open the side door after I get settled. You can find an empty room to stay in until after the service. I'll let Richard know what's going on, and he can see you after the service."

"Sounds like a plan. One other thing, I know I took a stupid chance seeing you like this, but I couldn't wait any longer. I'm afraid the boys will give me away in their innocent excitement. We need to stop before we get any closer to the church and try to explain to them that they can't say anything about me."

She nodded in agreement and called the boys over.

Elias took them both by the hand and knelt down to their level, "Guys, there are some very bad guys who think I'm dead. If they find out about me, they will come after me again and maybe take your mother too. You can't say anything to anyone about me, ok?"

"Ok," they both said in unison.

He saw puzzled confusion in their eyes, but they would do anything for their mother and him. He hugged them both and said a prayer that he wouldn't be betrayed by their innocence.

He turned to Abby, and said, "I'll walk on ahead and wait for you to unlock the side door."

She nodded and took the boys by their hands and continued the journey.

He turned into the sidewalk beside the church and leaned against the side of the church out of view. He heard faint voices as the small congregation shuffled into the main entrance above and to the left of him. He smiled, relieved to hear the banter of the boys as they raced up the steps like they always did.

It seemed forever before he heard the click of the panic bar on the door and saw it open slightly. He grabbed the handle and swung it wide enough to slip in. His eyes briefly met Abby's as she moved back to her boys in the classroom. He hesitated long enough to get his bearings.

He walked down a hall. His footsteps echoed in the silence as he ducked into an empty room. Through a speaker, he could hear the organist playing for the morning worship. He sat in an overstuffed rocker. Toys strewn around beckoned the clumsy advances of toddlers unsteady in their movements, always exploring and moving, slobbering, and learning. The room was empty with the foreboding of a dying church.

He couldn't help himself. The soft chair and his recovery mode put his lights out. He woke at the invitation hymn. He waited and listened. When he was sure the church was empty, he peeked out of his lair. He heard footsteps come down the stairs. It was Richard Wesley.

"Elias," he called out.

Elias came out into the main room and greeted him.

"I need to talk to you about committing to Christ and being baptized. Can we walk?"

Abby stayed in the locked church with the boys playing in the playroom as Elias and Richard walked in the early afternoon sun. Elias recounted his story to Richard as they walked.

When he finished he asked, "Will you baptize me? I can't have it recorded anywhere except my heart and God's book."

"Those are the only places that it matters. Of course, I will."

"One other thing, I am going to ask Abby to marry me. Will you perform the ceremony if she says yes?"

Richard said a silent prayer of praise under his breath. The past few months of persecution drove people from the church who needed it the most. He hadn't baptized anyone for as long as he could remember, and it was two years ago that he'd performed a marriage ceremony for someone. Discouraging doubt crept in his mind, constantly making him pray for strength and wisdom. This young man brought purpose and hope back with these simple requests.

"Yes, I will!" he said like a double agent in a spy movie.

He grinned inwardly at what Abby had confided in him earlier. Elias and Richard walked back to the church in silence to tell Abby of the pending transformation of Elias in baptism. They all agreed to ask Coy and Birdie to witness the event. They were the only people Elias trusted in New Detroit. The time was set for three forty-five, Monday afternoon, so Abby and the boys could be there.

They walked out of the side door of the church with the boys back to Abby's Place, each clinging to the other as if to make up for the time he was away. Abby unlocked the door and the boys raced inside. She went upstairs to change, but the boys clung to

Elias. He checked for listening devices. When he was certain he had found all of them, he slid into the booth with one boy on each side of him. When he was sure she was out of earshot, he motioned the boys into a huddle.

"Boys, I need to ask you if it would be ok to ask your mother to marry me."

Their eyes got big, and Duane spoke up, "Does that mean that you would be our father for real?"

"Yes, it would!"

They jumped on him in unison from both sides, excitedly mauling him in their exuberance.

"I'll need your help to pull this off."

He was trying his best to get control before Abby returned.

"I want to get your mother to invite Grandma for my baptism tomorrow. When she calls, I'll distract your mom. Duane, when she gives you the phone to talk to Grandma, walk upstairs with the phone and tell your grandma what's going on, so she will want to be there."

"What can I do?" said James, hurt he wasn't the chosen one.

"You follow Duane upstairs and stand as lookout to make sure your mom can't hear."

Satisfied he was a part of the conspiracy, James agreed.

"Now, when your mother returns, you have to act natural, so she won't suspect anything."

They were both trying to contain their excitement when Abby came back down. She knew something was up between her boys. Moms always know.

"Boys, go upstairs and change so we can eat."

They ran upstairs, glad to be away from Mom's scrutiny. This was really going to be tough. They had never succeeded in keeping anything from their mother, but this was really important, and they were glad to be in on the conspiracy.

When they were out of sight, Abby gave Elias the look that asked, "What's going on?" but he ignored her probe.

"I thought we could go to the Mexican restaurant down the street for lunch, if that is all right with you," he managed, changing the subject.

Her penetrating gaze eased as she replied, "Sure, sounds good."

She knew that eventually the boys would spill the beans.

The noisy descent announced the boys' arrival as they clamored toward Elias vying for position. They couldn't look their mother in the eye. She could shoot that dreaded truth serum across the room. If they came in contact with it, they knew they didn't stand a chance. They hid behind Elias, tugging on his fingers as they all made their way to the door.

After they ordered the food, the boys started hounding Elias to take them to the park after they ate. He raised his shirt slightly to reveal some of the multicolored bruises and scrapes on his body.

"I don't feel up to it today, boys."

Abby looked on in shock as he recounted his escape to freedom. It sounded like a science fiction tale when he explained about the Eagles. The boys sat disappointed, fidgeting, half listening.

By the time they got back to Abby's Place, Elias was ready to sit and rest. He didn't have the stamina to roughhouse with the boys. He sat in his favorite booth with Duane and James beside him.

"Do you think your mother would like to come tomorrow? I've never met her, and it would be nice for the boys to see her."

She thought for a minute. "I've talked about you a lot. She might be able to; she seems to be feeling well lately."

She took out her phone and called. They talked pleasantries and mother-daughter things for a while, then Abby asked, "Mom, would you like to come tomorrow afternoon and see Elias be baptized? Yes, he's the one I always talk about."

She shot an embarrassed glance to Elias, smiling. Duane danced around to her side of the booth and whispered repeatedly to his mother, "Can I talk? Can I talk? Can I talk?"

His mother fended off his advances toward the phone with her free hand.

"Duane wants to talk to you, Mom," she said, relinquishing the phone.

He grabbed the phone and struggled out of the booth toward the stairs with James close behind like a blocker fending off the opposing team so his ball carrier could score a touchdown. They both disappeared up the stairs.

"Alone at last!"

He took Abby's hand in his and kissed the back of it. She turned her full attention to him as she gazed into his eyes.

"There was a time when I wasn't sure I was going to make it back to you," he confessed, taking in the moment.

Too soon the boys prattled down the stairs. Duane handed the phone to his mom.

"Grandma wants to talk to you . . . here."

He abruptly handed the phone back to his mom and gave Elias a twinkle-in-the-eye look before he turned to run full tilt up the stairs before the secret involuntarily exploded from his mouth. James followed.

When Abby finished the call, Elias again took her hand. They basked in each other's company in silence, they were past words now. He hoped she would say yes tomorrow when he asked for her hand.

The shadows were disappearing to darkness outside when Elias said his long goodbye to Abby. He walked to the bus stop to catch a ride to Envirowheels and the Eagle. He had somewhere he wanted to go before his new life in Christ began tomorrow.

He made his way to the Eagle and lifted off into the darkness. A half hour later he set down gently in a meadow surrounded by woods.

In the darkness, he disappeared into the woods. It was his sanctuary; the place he went when he was on the cusp of a new life. He walked in starlight or moonlight, disturbed only by the night creatures foraging for food. He gained strength from the knowledge that God was in control and his family was safe in God's bosom. He made peace with himself and prayed for guidance and wisdom in whatever he was called to do. Out of tragedy came deliverance. He slept.

CHAPTER 21

The New Life

As the sun was peeking over the trees, he prepared the Eagle to depart. He said a prayer of praise for letting him have the opportunity to grieve and put his demons and doubts to rest. His new life beckoned as the old faded in the distance.

The time grew near for his immersion. Instead of landing the Eagle on the Envirowheels roof, he headed to Abby's neighborhood. Carefully he maneuvered the craft to the top of Abby's building and landed gently on the roof. He left the machine fully operational, so it would support its own weight. He wasn't sure of the structural integrity of the old building. He climbed down the maintenance ladder onto the fire escape and made his way to the street. He kept checking his pocket for the little box he had purchased earlier in the day. He hoped she would say yes.

He walked briskly past Abby's to the church office entrance and knocked. Pastor Richard appeared and let him in. They shook hands and exchanged pleasantries.

"I'm on my way to get Coy and Birdie in the church van. They don't live far, but their health prevents them from walking."

"Could I use your computer while you are gone?"

"Sure, just don't take down any world powers while I'm gone!" Richard said grinning, alluding to the story Elias recounted of the Rothfellas.

Elias settled in to apply for a marriage license. He found the proper site and input all the information. He typed in Alias Tobias Montague. He grinned. That one "typo" would stymie the computers and bury their license along with the others and not raise a red flag. In seconds, he had the certificate on the church computer. When the ceremony was over, they would apply their fingerprints to the screen and be legally married.

Richard returned with Coy and Birdie. Abby and the boys came in the side doors with a woman he had never met but knew instantly. He saw Abby in her face.

"Mother, I would like you to meet Elias Tobias Montague. Elias, meet my mother, Arlayne Vandevender."

He looked at her puzzled.

"Oh," she exclaimed, when she realized his confusion about the last name. "I took back my maiden name when my husband was killed to protect us after the riots."

Elias stuck out his hand to shake Arlayne's. He was unsure of the protocol involved and unsure how she would receive him.

"So, you're the man who has given my daughter such happiness and heartache."

She let him squirm for a second with his hand in midair before she brushed it aside and came in for a hug. Elias's apprehension melted, and he hugged her back.

"Now, let me play with my grandchildren."

With that she grabbed the boys' hands and disappeared into the playroom. Abby moved in for a caress and a kiss. They stayed as one, still not caught up on their need for each other.

Richard poked his head around the corner and admonished Elias to get ready. Elias put on the robe provided and walked down into the baptistery where Richard was waiting, unaware of the people gathered to witness the event. He repeated the proper words, and Richard laid him back gently until he was totally immersed. Everyone present cheered. He came out of the water euphoric in the fact that he was following in his father's footsteps and doing the will of his heavenly father.

It was just water; why did he feel so changed?

After toweling off and putting on dry clothes, he prepared to go greet those close to him. He had a mission to accomplish. He patted the small box in his pocket as he walked up the stairs to his new life.

The people lined the aisle to hug him or give him encouragement. Abby hung back, wanting to have his total attention when she met him for the first time after his transformation. Elias was surprised to see Darious and Florinda and even Jake Tanner. They were all beaming!

Abby stood in front of him. He looked into her eyes, took her hand, and led her to the front of the church.

"I've been wanting to ask you this for a long time but until this moment I have been unworthy of such a beautiful, intelligent, caring woman," he said, looking deeply into her eyes and getting down on one knee. "Abby, will you marry me?"

The church was hushed in anticipation of her reply.

"I'm not letting you go off and get yourself blown up in some foreign land without me ever again, no matter what the excuse!" she replied with her finger pointed right at his heart and fire in her eyes. "Yes, I'll marry you! Right now!"

The church erupted; the boys ran down the aisle and danced around the embracing couple. Her mother wiped a tear and Birdie took out her handkerchief just as Coy grabbed her hand.

Elias didn't hear all the commotion. He was in a place in his soul that he had never been. Feeble words failed to describe. He sensed that this was where humans were created to be, but sin and Satan had turned their hearts.

Abby pulled away and put her hand up, palm toward the gathering. The room fell silent.

"We've got a lot of wedding planning to do."

She went to Birdie and asked if she would stand with her as matron of honor. The two waitresses who still worked with her were bridesmaids.

Elias took her lead and asked Darious to be his best man and Jake to be his groomsman. He brought the boys over in a huddle and asked them to stand with the other men and be groomsmen also. He bent down and addressed James especially.

"I need you to hold these rings and give them to me when I give you the signal. Can you handle that?"

The little boy's eyes got big at such a responsibility. He stretched out his hand, palm up, to receive the rings. He put his other hand on top, so the box couldn't escape. Florinda walked over to the organ and started practicing the wedding songs Abby had requested.

Abby went over to Coy and asked, "Would you walk me down the aisle?"

"I would be honored, Abby."

The stage was set. After a dry run, they all got in position for the real thing. Florinda started playing the organ. Elias could not believe he was getting married to the love of his life. As she came down the aisle, he imagined the church filled with his extended family. His family was sitting in the front row, his mother shedding a tear and his father beaming. He smiled at the thought. He knew they would have both loved Abby and the boys.

Elias only remembered the part of the wedding where he put the ring on Abby's finger and the part where Richard said, "You may kiss the bride!"

When they got to the back of the church for the receiving line, Elias had to ask her, "Abby, how did all these people get here. Did someone give my secret away?"

"No, no one told me what you had in mind. If you hadn't asked me to marry you, I was going to ask you, and I wasn't going to take no for an answer! You are not going to get yourself blown up ever again without me!"

She had her index finger pointed right at his heart as she talked and had fire in her eyes again. The wedding participants gathered around to congratulate the new couple. Abby raised her hand and when the din in the room diminished, she invited everyone to the basement for cake and punch.

"You were pretty sure of yourself, weren't you?" grinned Elias.

"Yep!"

When all the guests left, the new family made their way back to Abby's Place. The sun was disappearing behind the skyline when Abby unlocked the door for the last time. The boys ran upstairs to play, leaving the newlyweds to themselves.

"I can't stay around here, Abby. Someone is bound to recognize me. We have a research facility in New Mexico that has a house we can live in until I know what direction God takes me."

"I know, Darious talked about that when I invited them to the wedding. Elias, it doesn't matter where we go as long as we are together. Because the government took my dream away, I have no ties here. I've felt trapped in its vision for me, which is not mine."

Elias was relieved to hear that. "I don't know exactly how much Darious has told you about what we do, but come with me, I want to show you."

They headed up the stairs past Abby's apartment to the access stairs to the roof. Elias took her hand and helped her up the last few steps, so she could unlock the door. The stars were out by the time they opened the door into the night air. The sounds of the city below added to the ambiance as they gazed at the sky. He led her to the back of the building in the starlight glow.

She didn't immediately see the craft in the dim light, but she heard the soft hum of the engine and felt the lightness of the air after a rain. A sense of well-being wrapped around them as they approached. Elias touched the craft and a stairway appeared.

Only then did Abby realize there was an aircraft parked on the roof of her apartment. She was a little afraid as he took her hand.

"Your chariot awaits, my queen!" Elias said as he led her up the ramp. "These are the most advanced flying machines humans have ever known."

"I didn't see any wings. How does it fly?"

"That explanation will take a long time. You'll just have to trust me that it's safe. One like it got me all the way to Dubai and back safely. We need to disappear tonight. Can we do that?"

"Yes, we can. The boys are going to absolutely love this thing!"

She said a silent prayer for safe travels as she came down the ramp to embark on their new life. They spent the next three hours packing what the ship could carry and loading it so there would also be room for them.

When they finished packing, she took her keys, her cell phone, and her bit-coin card and placed then neatly on the counter in what used to be her dream. She looked around one last time and hurried up the stairs.

The boys were asleep on their beds. They were as exhausted as she was after such a long day. She had everything they would need already packed when she roused them out of bed.

"Boys, get up! Elias has a surprise for you."

She gently shook them awake and took them by the hands up the access stairs. They were still groggy when they reached the top of the stairs where Elias greeted them. He took them by their hands and guided them around to where the Eagle was perched. The only light was a faint glow coming from the computer monitor as it showed the preflight check progress. The boys boarded the craft thinking it was a dream. It looked like a spaceship!

Elias strapped them in their seats. He showed Abby how to swivel the seat beside him and strap in. Elias strapped in and prepared to take off. Abby shot an excited, apprehensive look at each of the boys, like she did when she was strapped in to a roller coaster. They were smiling in excited anticipation as Elias slowly lifted off and retracted the landing gear. He touched the monitor and the lights of the city came on the screen.

"Wow!" exclaimed the boys as they watched in wide-eyed wonderment.

The lights went by slowly until the craft reached cruising altitude. Elias couldn't resist showboating a little. He manually rolled the control forward quickly. The Eagle responded instantly, pinning everyone back in their seats with so much force that no one could even talk. They were so excited, they were a little frightened. No roller coaster or amusement park ride could rival the thrill of an Eagle ride with Elias!

As they were settling into their new life, Comrade was opening the front door of Abby's Place. She walked in to silence; usually Abby had the coffee on and everything ready for customers by now. She walked up the stairs, yelling Abby's name. The place was empty. She would have to report the disappearance to her superiors, not a good thing for her status in the party.

She kicked an abandoned toy down the stairs in anger. Why don't these people see that everything the party does is for the good of the people? She saw the keys, the phone, and the bit-card on the counter. She grabbed the bit-card. She'd earned it for all the grief Abby just put her through.

CHAPTER 22

The Fingerprint of Faith

Abby walked into Elias's office to tell him breakfast was ready. He couldn't help putting his hand on her protruding belly as he pulled her onto his lap and kissed her. Sometimes he got to feel the baby kick. It had been a year since they'd left New Detroit and settled in New Mexico.

He marveled at how Abby took charge of the household and the finances and how she grasped the needs of everyone in the camp and always seemed somehow to get those needs met, all while growing this little human inside her body. She could do anything. She completed him. She seemed to understand when he got up in the night to walk and think and pray.

In the stillness of the night, he would walk through Abby's garden in the moonlight and the starlight when a vision would wake him, disturbed only by the night creatures on an eternal quest for survival. A quest joined now by Christians who were made scapegoats and enemies for every shortfall and problem in the world.

The Beast was consolidating his power. Nation after nation fell under his spell in a world gone mad. His evil need to feed off the fear of his followers led to the persecution and be-heading of believers who showed no fear. All who refused the mark were sentenced to death.

Elias was troubled at first for he could not understand. Abby pointed out to him his faith was being tested. As he relaxed and turned control of his life to God, he began to comprehend. Unlike Moses, who led the Israelites to a promised land, he was to make it possible for the believers in Christ to hide in plain sight in the coming apocalyptic events, before Christ's Second Coming. He now realized his purpose for learning the Bible as a child. The Word admonishes believers to always be ready for the Second Coming. No hidden secret was imbedded to show the exact time. The practice of assigning numbers to scriptures was to show how the faithful were to survive and thrive, even as boils and sores consumed the bodies of those who begged for death but could not die.

Out of his research was born the bitchain. The same silica-based paper, which Sanddollar produced and he had used for his fingerprint security, was imbedded with beautiful murals. People were drawn to them. When a believer touched the paper, the mural turned to a picture of Jesus on the Cross who died for all. Their fingerprints of faith connected them with all other faithful. A sense of well-being and the knowledge that they were not alone washed over them. They instinctively gathered with other believers in the knowledge they would be redeemed.

For the first time in the history of humankind, the true nature of a person's heart was revealed. A nonbeliever, with the mark of the beast, would see a beautiful mural and discard the paper on his way to his own destruction.

Believers were disappearing all over the world. They flocked to some of the most inhospitable places on earth, where they found safety and sustenance through the power that the Eagles produced. Clear, clean water sprang forth from the earth wherever they gathered. Food was plentiful, even though they didn't bear the mark of the beast. They seemed to be invisible, like the Eagles in flight. God was at work.

As Noah built an ark for the redemption of the few after the flood, Elias toiled to produce the Eagles and the bitchain for the redemption of the many in the end times. The bitchain was incorporated into the control brain of the Eagles. They seemed to know where to go to redeem the most precious thing that God had created—the souls of man. Thousands upon thousands of Eagles were in service with more being produced every day.

Elias had never and would never sell one of Darious's Eagles, yet the company flourished. They operated in the mountains and the deserts, yet they were protected. The small colonies of believers spread throughout the world. They were ready. Please, come, Lord Jesus!

Back Cover

What if God's children are not "raptured" from this earth? What if they are protected as God protected his chosen people, Israel, so they will prosper and repopulate the earth in the thousand-year reign of Christ? He provides the way for the remnant to survive by using broken people as he always has!

Acknowledgments

I would like to thank my four daughters Jody, Michele, Tracy, and Ashley for their encouragement. They love the old stories and help prod me through the difficult times of self doubt.

Joni Wilson mentored me through the editing process and actually made this old storyteller sound like some kind of a writer. Bless You.

There are many illustrators, graphic design people and countless people that work behind the scenes to make a book happen> I would like to thank these people who I probably will never meet. They are all a member of the Best Selling Publishing team who makes this all happen. Thank You.

Thank You

Thank you for reading my book. If you enjoyed it,
please take a moment to leave me a review.

About the Author

The author lives in Indiana with his wife of fifty years Suzanne. Together they raised four daughters and are in the process of spoiling three grandchildren. Daniel likes to garden and enjoys sharing his delicious sweet corn every season with neighbors and friends. He has been to Cuba with Living In Faith ministries installing water systems and distributing Bibles to the churches. It has become his passion to get Bibles to the Cuban churches. Through his first book God's Will In Cuba he has raised enough money to ensure that a case of Bibles can be distributed to every church where a water filtration system is installed.

In his retirement he likes to write novels and short stories. enjoy his stories at daniellfultonwritingforyou.com

Discover Other Titles
by Daniel Fulton

God's Will in Cuba

COMING SOON:
THE BEAST

Hate is not the opposite of love. Hate is a twin to love; both born out of passion and separated by one chromosome called perception.

The opposite of love is fear. He was incapable of love or compassion. His actions were governed by the need for humans to fear and worship him.

It gave him total control. He used it to manipulate the mind and pervert the morals and ultimately control the destiny of humanity!

Connect with Me

At daniellfultonwritingforyou.com

Made in the USA
San Bernardino, CA
14 December 2019